FROZEN STIFF

A Chase Adams FBI Thriller
Book 1

Patrick Logan

Books by Patrick Logan

Detective Damien Drake
Book 1: Butterfly Kisses
Book 2: Cause of Death
Book 3: Download Murder
Book 4: Skeleton King
Book 5: Human Traffic
Book 6: Drug Lord: Part One
Book 7: Drug Lord: Part Two
Book 8: Prized Fight

Dr. Beckett Campbell, ME
Book 0: Bitter End
Book 1: Organ Donor
Book 2: Injecting Faith
Book 3: Surgical Precision

Chase Adams FBI Thrillers
Book 1: Frozen Stiff
Book 2: Shadow Suspect
Book 3: Drawing Dead
Book 4: Amber Alert
Book 4.5: Georgina's Story
Book 5: Dirty Money
Book 6: Devil's Den

This book is a work of fiction. Names, characters, places, and incidents in this book are either entirely imaginary or are used fictitiously. Any resemblance to actual people, living or dead, or of places, events, or locales is entirely coincidental.

Copyright © Patrick Logan 2017
Interior design: © Patrick Logan 2017
All rights reserved.

This book, or parts thereof, cannot be reproduced, scanned, or disseminated in any print or electronic form.

First Edition: January 2019

Prologue

"You can't get away from this, Chase! Why don't you just come back up here and we can talk about it, face-to-face!"

Chase Adams winced and scrambled along the side of the hill, pressing her back against the snow-covered surface as she moved.

The man was standing on the road above, roughly fifteen feet up, and if he saw her, she knew that the next bullet wouldn't be in her side, but in her skull.

Talk about it... what a joke.

Through gritted teeth, she tried to keep her pain at bay while shuffling, grateful for both the cover of darkness provided by the trees and the sound of the wind whistling between their branches.

It was a cold afternoon, and the frigid air nipped at her even through the thick red parka that covered her from knees to chin. Wind entered the bullet hole in the right side, causing it to puff up and make her movements even more awkward.

"Chase! Chaaaaaase!" The voice had a singsong quality to it now.

The bastard was enjoying this.

Chase made it to an exposed culvert jutting from the side of the hill, and with a soft grunt, lowered herself beneath it.

Please don't look down here... please just get back in your car and leave.

Somewhere in the distance she heard the chime from a car, an indication that a door had been left ajar. A quick glance in that direction confirmed that it was coming from the battered teal-colored sedan that she had stolen at gunpoint. Based on the way the hood was curled around an ancient oak tree, she was surprised that she had managed to crawl out of it relatively unscathed.

Chase could see blood on the cracked leather seats even from her vantage point nearly twenty feet away, but that was from *before*, that was from the bullet embedded in her right side, just above her hip.

Please… just leave.

"I'll tell you what, Chase, come out now, and I'll make it quick—I promise. It won't be like the others. But if I have to come down there and find you, which I will—you know I will—then it'll be bad."

So much for talking.

Chase squeezed her eyes together tightly, and allowed herself several deep breaths. The pain in her side had dulled considerably since the hotel, and after collecting herself, she finally gathered the nerve to look down at the hand clutching her side.

Beneath the pale spears of light that eked between the trees, her small fingers appeared smeared with a thick, purple substance.

Chase ground her teeth, steeled herself, and then pulled her hand away from the spot just above her right hip.

Down feather insulation clung to the blood-covered hole, and after first trying, and then failing, to clear them completely to allow a clear view of the wound, Chase gave up and slowly unzipped the coat to peer inside.

The hole in her shirt was ragged, and the shirt, a white blouse, was filthy and nearly completely covered in blood.

The bullet hole itself was rimmed with black, burnt fabric.

Chase covered the wound with her frigid hand and applied pressure. A hiss exited her mouth, and she froze.

"Chase... *Chaaaaaaaaaase*! Come out, come out wherever you are!"

With all of her prodding, the pain had intensified, but she knew there was still one more thing to check: she had to inspect her back.

Chase inhaled deeply, and held her breath, before pulling away from the side of the hill. It was risky, but she had to know.

Just a glance...

A second later, Chase collapsed against the embankment, breathing heavily, eyes closed once more.

The bullet had gone completely through.

Something in the back of her mind, her police training perhaps, her time as first a Seattle PD Narcotics officer, then as an NYPD Detective, told her that this was a good thing. That if the bullet was still lodged inside her, it would continue to do damage until it was removed.

But this realization did nothing to soothe her pain.

Through or not, if she didn't get help soon, Chase would bleed out. Then it wouldn't matter if the bullet was lodged in her side, her chest, her heart, or her brain.

She tightened her grip on the gun clutched in her free hand.

"Agent Adams, I'm getting bored of this," as if to reinforce the point, the lilt in his voice disappeared. "I'll tell you what... new deal: you come out right now, and I won't kill your husband and son."

Chase's eyes snapped open, and her mouth went slack.

No, he can't—

As if reading her thoughts, the man continued, "Oh, that's right. I know all about little Felix and Brad. You see, Chase, I've been at this a long time. A long, *long* time, and you don't stick around in this game by not knowing everything… everything about my victims. About what you guys did to her."

Chase closed her eyes again, only this time it wasn't from the pain, but from a realization. She ground her teeth so hard that a fine powder rained down on her tongue.

A game… that's all this is to him, a sick, twisted game of revenge. But for what? What the hell did we do?

"Last chance, Chase. Come out now, hands up, or Felix and Brad die before you do. Last… chance…"

PART I – Trying to Walk

TWO WEEKS AGO

Chapter 1

CHASE EYED THE MAN in the driver seat sporting aviator sunglasses that were too big even for his large features. His elbow was hanging casually out the window, and cold air wafted to them from inside the van.

"You girls need a ride?" he said with a slight grin.

Chase turned to her sister, at the sheen covering her button nose, the soft skin beneath her eyes. It was hot, too hot, and they still had at least two miles to cover before they got home.

"We're fine," Chase said forcefully. She grabbed her sister's hand and tugged her along.

To her dismay, the man in the van kept pace.

"You sure? It's awfully hot out here."

Chase looked over at the driver, and was surprised to see that his smile had widened.

A sudden buzzing, a thick, droning sound, bombarded Chase's ears and she felt momentarily dizzy.

He's right. It's so hot out here. When's the last time we had something to drink? Was it the water? No, it was... oh, it was the syrupy Snocone... that was it. And mama said that those drinks will only make you more *thirsty.*

"I said, we're fine," she snapped.

The man opened his mouth to reply, but the only sound he made was more of that strange buzzing. It seemed to be inside her skull now, as if her brain had been replaced by a wasp nest.

To her right, her sister was saying something and tugging her hand, probably telling her that they should, please, just take the ride, but Chase didn't hear any words. All she heard was that damn buzzing, that incessant—

***

Chase's eyes snapped open, her mouth parting in a gasp. Her body was covered in sweat, an uncomfortable stickiness that coated her arms, her chest, her legs.

Finally managing a full breath, she saw fog form in front of her face. Despite the sweat, she shivered, her gaze moving to the open window.

It was frigid inside her small apartment and—

Bzzzzz

Chase's eyes went from the window to her phone on the bedside table. As she stared at it, it buzzed again, the vibrations moving it toward the edge.

Chase grabbed it before it fell.

The number was unlisted, but she answered anyway.

"Hello?" she asked, then cleared her throat when her voice came out hoarse and cracking.

What time is it?

"Alaska," the male voice on the other end of the line said. Unlike her own, it was clear, distinct, not groggy with sleep.

"What?"

"Alaska. Head to the airport—flight leaves in two hours. Tickets are at the desk under your name. Bring the badge and gun that Agent Stitts gave you. Don't be late."

Chase sat bolt upright.

This was the call she was waiting for. She hadn't expected it to be so obtuse, cryptic, and informal, but that didn't matter. It was *the* call.

"I'm up, sir," she said, but the other end of the line had already gone dead.

Chase put the phone back on the bedside table and rubbed the last vestiges of sleep from her eyes.

Then, when her vision was completely clear, she turned to the clock.

It was four-fifteen in the morning.

Her eyes naturally moved to the photograph beside the clock next, the one of Brad resting on a knee, a smile on his bearded face. His arm was wrapped around Felix's shoulders, resting on his brightly colored backpack.

The photo had been taken three years ago on little Felix's first day of school.

Chase reached out with two fingers and pressed them gently on the glass.

Then she rose, grabbed the bag that she had packed months ago from the foot of her bed, confirmed that her pistol and FBI badge rested on top, and started to dress.

Chapter 2

"THERE ARE NO DIRECT flights from JFK to Anchorage," the sulking woman at the flight desk informed Chase. "Your connection is in Seattle, and you best be hurrying, the flight is boarding real soon."

Chase nodded and hurried to the security desk. She flashed her FBI badge, and then told the TSA agent that she had a pistol to check.

"Yeah, we're going to have to take you and your gun to security to check it over," the man in the uniform informed her in a slow drawl. He was going on sixty and had thin, coppery hair. Chase considered that his hair might have been dyed to match his nicotine stained mustache.

"I've got a flight to catch," she said with a frown. "Can we just hurry it up?"

The man eyed her up and down, taking in the full length of her black suit, the white blouse beneath. He did so in the creepiest way possible, and Chase bit back a scathing retort.

The man's leer suddenly broke into a grin.

"Hey, aren't you that Police Sergeant that told the women of New York to be bitches?"

Chase's scowl became a sneer.

Just my luck, I get the only asshole who remembers that.

Her mind flicked back to the day that she had stood atop the podium, then acting as NYPD Sergeant of the 62nd precinct. Her goal had been to prevent more women from being murdered, from their lips being painted red with blood.

FBI Agent Jeremy Stitts had been in the crowd then, looking up at her. And with all eyes on her, she had gone ahead and said pretty much exactly what the TSA douchebag before her had just repeated.

Use your gut, your instincts, Agent Stitts had instructed her, and her gut told her to inform New York, especially the women, to look out for themselves.

That had been more than six months ago; more than half a year had passed since she was the active Sergeant of 62nd precinct, and she had thought that it was all behind her.

Just my luck to meet the one man in New York who remembers...

The TSA Agent's eyes flicked to the FBI badge that Chase still held open in one hand.

"Didn't work out that good for ya, did it?" There was a twinkle in the man's eyes that made Chase want to punch him. But that was what *he* wanted, too, she realized.

Instead, she put on her most patronizing expression.

"I'll be sure to put a good word in for you when Walmart comes looking for a new security guard."

The man stopped smiling.

"Off to the right," he barked. "Cops, FBI, POTUS. Don't matter. All guns must be inspected prior to boarding."

Chase followed the man's nicotine stained fingers toward a door marked SECURITY CHECK. Her only chance of making the flight now was if she was the only one in there.

***

Huffing, her lungs and legs burning, Chase made it to the gate just as the agent was announcing last call over the loud speaker.

"Wait!" she hollered as she approached. "I'm here! *Wait!*"

The gate attendant turned her back to her as if she didn't hear, and started toward the door, pulling a keycard from her hip as she did.

You've got to be kidding me.

The security check hadn't been empty; it had been *packed*. Her only saving grace was that she knew one of the inspectors, a cousin of Detective Simmons whom she had worked with back in 62nd precinct, and he had fast-laned her.

And yet, even after all of this bureaucratic bullshit, the woman was still going to close the door on her.

She was going to miss her flight.

Chase sprinted and somehow managed to slip a foot in the door before the gate attendant could close it completely.

The woman, who at this point, Chase was convinced was some sort of android, continued to shut the door despite the presence of her foot.

It was heavy, and she winced when it pinched her Jimmy Choos.

"I'm here," she huffed, holding the ticket out for the woman to see. The woman's eyes moved from the ticket to Chase's foot, then back to her face.

"Only this time," she said sternly, as if she were offering parole to a two-time offender in a three-strike state. She snatched the ticket from Chase's hand, and then scanned the barcode with the handheld reader.

Chase wanted to come back with something witty, snarky, but she was too out of breath to say anything.

Which was probably for the best.

The woman pulled the door open just wide enough for Chase to slip through, and she hurried down the runway, a slight limp to her gait until the pain in her foot subsided.

Just when she thought her day couldn't get any worse, Chase discovered that her ticket had her sandwiched between two men who looked like long-lost relatives of Jabba the Hut.

12   LOGAN

Even at a hair over a hundred pounds, coming in at a generous five-foot four, Chase's shoulders were so tightly squeezed between them that her breathing was restricted.

Thankfully, it was six a.m., and she was exhausted from her interrupted sleep and the run to and throughout JFK, and Chase managed to pass out even before the plane left the ground.

***

"Suit yourself, but it's awfully hot out there. And in here—" the man gestured toward the interior of the minivan. As he did, a blast of cold air struck Chase in the face, even though she was standing more than three feet away. "—it's nice."

And there it was again, the charming smile, the comfortable, unassuming pose with his arm dangling out the window.

Chase wanted to get in the car, **really** wanted to, and she could tell by the way that her sister kept tugging on her hand, that she wanted to get in too.

Chase turned her eyes to the sun, squinting at the near impossible brightness.

"Suit yourself," the man repeated.

Chase looked back just in time to see the man's tinted window close before he sped off, tires squealing.

"C'mon, Chase, it's soooo hot," her sister whined. "Why can't we take the ride? He looks nice."

Chase stopped and then squatted so that she was at eye level with her sister. Chase was only two years older, but Georgina was a good foot shorter than she was.

She grasped her sister's shoulders tightly.

"Not everyone who offers you a ride is a good person, Georgie. There are some people out there…"

Her sentence trailed off as her mind began to wander.

"You're hurting me," Georgina whined, as she squirmed beneath Chase's grip.

Chase let go of her and stood.

"Sorry," she grumbled. "Let's go. It's hot, and I'm thirsty."

Chapter 3

"Ma'am?" a hand shook her shoulder. "Ma'am? You okay?"

Chase opened her eyes, and then startled, confused by her surroundings.

The stewardess leaned away from her.

"I'm sorry, but we landed five minutes ago. I'm not sure if you have a connecting flight or…"

Chase blinked, then realized that she was in an airplane and that it must have landed in Seattle. Part of her mind tried to tell her that this was a dream, but she knew better.

The other thing, the thing with her sister, *that* had been a dream.

Sort of.

"Sorry," she grumbled. "Must have fallen asleep."

The woman stood up straight and smiled.

"That's alright. It was an early flight—I would have fallen asleep myself if I didn't have to work."

Chase nodded, and then undid her seatbelt. Now, without an ogre hanging on each of her shoulders, she could finally take a full breath, and did so in earnest.

"Thanks," she grumbled. She stood, stretched her calves, then checked her watch. It was close to lunchtime, and she had an hour or so to kill before boarding the final leg of her journey to Anchorage.

Chase collected her bag from the overhead compartment.

"Will my checked baggage be automatically transferred, or do I need to pick it up?"

The stewardess, who was busy checking all of the overhead bins for forgotten carry-ons, said, "It should go directly to your final destination. But I'd check with the boarding agent at the next flight just to be sure."

Chase thanked the woman again and disembarked.

Ten minutes later, she found herself sitting in the busy food court, cramming over-salted French fries into her mouth, and watching whatever passed as cheese these days melt from the heat of the microwaved hamburger patty and drip onto the greasy plastic.

She chased the fries with a sip from her Coke.

Not the way I imagined it...

For a split second, she debated calling up some of her old colleagues from her time as a Narcotics Officer here in Seattle, but quickly squashed this idea.

It wasn't worth the memories, drudging up a past that would only serve to reopen old wounds.

She had spent a good three years as a Narc; the fourth, and what was to be her final year, was blurred by an addiction that still scarred the inside of her arms to this day.

Definitely best to just sit and eat this burger alone, chase it with the syrupy soft drink, and prepare for Anchorage.

The problem with this, however, was that she had no idea what or who she was preparing for. For as long as she could remember, Chase wanted to be part of the FBI, but could never see a way to transition from law enforcement to the Bureau. That is until her brief stint as NYPD Sergeant of the 62nd precinct. In her first and only case—the so-called Download Killer, a disgruntled housewife who murdered young women, painted their lips with their blood, and then published stories about their deaths online—she had immediately brought in the FBI to lend a hand.

FBI Special Agent Jeremy Stitts had helped her solve that case, and in the process, Chase had gained insight into why her application kept being overlooked. Stitts had spent a good deal of time observing her leading up to Ryanne Elliot's untimely death, and Chase couldn't help but shake the feeling that the entire case had been a sort of job interview.

And she had passed... or so she had thought. Agent Stitts had given her a badge and a service pistol, but instead of whisking her off to Quantico for training, he told her to sit tight, to wait for the call.

Chase wasn't good at sitting and waiting.

Too much time in her own head was never a good thing.

Too much time to remember.

It didn't help that after the Download Killer, she had come home to an empty house. Her husband Brad had taken their seven-year-old son Felix and had gone on an extended vacation with the boy.

It wasn't his fault, Chase knew. Brad had told her repeatedly that she put them second behind her job, and yet she had ignored him.

And then, poof, they were gone.

Even when she pleaded with Brad, even after she had resigned from the NYPD—granted she wasn't so much eased out the door as pushed through by Internal Affairs—he said he needed time.

That they both did.

In the interim, she could see Felix whenever she wanted, but it wasn't the same. Chase missed seeing his face every night, even if most of the time when she looked down on him he was already fast asleep in his bed.

It wasn't the same; they weren't a family anymore, and this saddened her deeply.

And it also reminded her of a past long before Seattle that she had worked hard to forget.

I'm doing it for you, Georgina... I'm doing all of this for you.

A month passed without a call from the Bureau, and Chase began to wonder.

Be patient, she chided herself. *They'll call.*

But when one month bled into two, she hadn't been able to resist the urge: Chase picked up the phone and dialed Agent Stitts.

The man told her the same thing that she had told herself: just sit tight and wait.

On the third month, just as she was considering appealing to her ex-partner and good friend Damien Drake to join his PI firm, if for nothing else than to pass the time, she finally got the call.

And, like the flight she just experienced, it wasn't what she had expected.

There was no private jet as she had seen countless times on Criminal Minds, no glass conference rooms filled with high-tech equipment and a team of slightly autistic yet brilliant specialists.

So far, it was just her, a douchebag TSA agent, an unhappy gate attendant, and two obese seat partners.

Oh, and the burger.

This burger.

Chase took a bite, and then dabbed at the grease that dribbled onto her chin.

She was nearly done with her meal when an announcement informed her that Delta flight 0199 to Anchorage was starting to board. After a short debate about whether or not she should finish her quarter pounder, and deciding against it, Chase took out her phone and scrolled to her recent calls.

All but one of the ten outgoing calls were to the same number. She dialed it now and waited until the answering machine picked up on the third ring.

"Hey, buddy, I hope you're having a great day at school. I'm just calling to let you know that I probably won't be seeing you this weekend." Chase closed her eyes and tilted her chin to the ceiling. She fought back the hitch that tried to claw its way into her throat. "I know I promised to take you to the indoor water park, but I can't this weekend. Mommy's going away for work… to Alaska! It's supposed to be super cold there, but I'll make sure to keep warm. I'll be sure to pick you up something nice, and I promise to take you to the water park when I get back. I love you, Felix. And I love you too, Brad. Talk soon. Chase."

Despite her best efforts, Chase was crying softly as she boarded the final flight of this leg of her journey.

Chapter 4

"**What do you mean** my luggage isn't here?" Chase demanded, feeling the effects of the long travel day already. That, mixed with the early wakeup time and the poor quality of what little sleep she had, was taking its toll on her, and she fought hard to keep her cool.

The man behind the counter, a creature with fish eyes and thin lips that stretched nearly all the way across his face, appeared to pick up on these cues and leaned away from the counter. She got the impression that the glass partition that separated them wasn't just for show.

"Ma'am, for some reason your luggage was held behind."

Chase felt her blood pressure rise.

"But my—" she leaned in close, "—my service pistol was in there!"

The man's eyes narrowed, and Chase produced her FBI badge that Agent Stitts had sent her.

Fish eyes blinked, seemed to extend toward the FBI seal, then retracted.

"Agent Adams, I'm not sure what to tell you, but your stuff isn't here. Pistol included. I'll make a note on your file stating that you are a government employee and hopefully…"

Chase drowned this banter out. She knew how it ended.

And yet, what little she heard touched a nerve.

Government employee? What am I? Some sort of aide to a local congressman?

She closed her eyes and breathed deeply.

"Is it there?" she said, cutting the man off mid-sentence.

"Excuse me?"

Chase opened her eyes.

"My stuff. Can you confirm that it's in Seattle? So far, you've only told me that it isn't here, in Anchorage. Did it leave New York?"

The man turned to his computer and pecked at the keyboard with two index fingers.

What seemed like hours later, he looked up.

"Nope," he said simply.

Chase scowled.

"No, what? No, it's not there or…?"

The man's thin lids slid over protruding eyeballs.

"No, I can't tell you. All I know is that your luggage was not put on the flight to Anchorage. Now, I'm sure your stuff will make it here tomorrow, or the next day." He spun a piece of paper around and slid it under the partition. "Now, if you'd be so kind as to put down the address of the place you'll be staying, I'll make sure they get it to you as soon as possible."

Chase's frown deepened as she looked over the sheet of paper, which asked for more personal information than an eHarmony profile.

Problem was, she had no idea where she was going to be staying. In fact, she really had no idea what the hell she was doing here at all.

Alaska, the voice on the phone had said. And that was pretty much it.

Aside from bringing her badge and gun, the latter of which had promptly gone missing.

Along with all of her clothes and a jacket appropriate for the weather.

Chase shook her head and filled out as much of the form as she could, making sure to write out her cell number twice, before handing it back.

The man looked at it, then at her. Everything he did seemed to be governed by how many times his giant eyeballs were covered with those translucent membranes. It was as if he needed to ask his eyes permission to breathe.

"Your address?" he said at last.

"Don't know where I'll be staying yet. But my number's there. Just call me when you get it."

More staring.

Chase sucked her teeth, fighting the urge to curse.

"Just call me; I need my pistol."

The man frowned, and when he turned to file her paper in a stack of two dozen others, Chase fled the booth before she said or did something that would ultimately end in the man *"losing"* her luggage form.

Her face was warm, her stomach full from the meal to the point of bursting, and she felt dizzy.

What a way to make a first impression.

She pressed by a middle-aged couple who were searching for their suitcase on the carousel, oddly dressed in Hawaiian shirts, and then she made her way toward the main lobby.

A peek at the wall of windows across the terminal drew an instinctive shiver: it was snowing outside, and Chase, always uncomfortable on airplanes, hadn't even worn a jacket. The only things she had brought in her carry-on was a small makeup case, her toothbrush, deodorant, a T-shirt, several pairs of underwear, and her hair straightener.

The rest had been packed neatly into the suitcase that had subsequently been left behind.

Chase shook her head and hurried away from the crowds. Truth be told, she hadn't a clue where she was going, but fueled by the frustration that this day had offered, she moved with purpose.

And a need for a drink.

Instead of alcohol, however, she settled for a small coffee cart from which she grabbed a Styrofoam cup full of caustic-looking fluid. She was in the process of putting on the lid, which, obviously, felt just a fraction of an inch too small, when a hand gently brushed her shoulder.

She jumped, and then slid her hips backwards to avoid the scalding liquid that cascaded to the floor.

Chase lost it.

"Jesus! Shit!" she said, spinning around. "Why the *fuck* would—"

A man in a dark navy suit with a narrow face and the beginnings of a blond goatee stood before her, shock and fear on his young face.

Chase glanced upward at the hat he was sporting—also navy, just a little lighter than the color of his suit—then at his hands.

Gripped in white fingers was a wipe board roughly the size of a sheet of paper. Written on it was a single word: ADAMS.

"I'm so sorry, ma'am. I just—"

Chase's eyes narrowed.

"Why do you have my name on your board?" she snapped.

The man looked down at his hands, then turned it around so that the word was the right way up. He did this in a manner that made Chase think that he had forgotten what he had written on it.

"A-A-A-Adams..." he mumbled to himself. "I thought that m-m-maybe—"

"Who are you?"

The man broke into a grin, and he held a hand out to her. Chase didn't shake it.

"I asked who you were."

The man's smile faded.

"F-F-F-Floyd. F-Floyd M-M-Montgomery. Are you Chase A-A-Adams? I s-s-seen a picture on the n-n-news a while back, s-s-something—"

Chase cut him off before he could finish recounting a story she knew all too well.

"Yes, I'm Chase Adams. What do you want?"

The man looked down again.

"I must have m-m-missed you getting off the p-plane. The gates changed at the last m-m-minute, and I hurried, I really d-d-did, but it's hard to—"

"What do you want?" Chase repeated, trying to save him the pain of forcing the words out with his stutter.

She saw his Adam's apple bob and he lowered his eyes before answering.

"I'm here to p-pick you up. Agent M-M-Martinez sent me to come g-g-g-get you."

Chapter 5

GIRDWOOD, MUNICIPALITY OF ANCHORAGE, *Alaska.*

Chase had never heard of the place before today, but quickly learned that it was a small town about forty miles from Anchorage with a population of roughly the same as an average housing complex in NYC: two thousand people.

In fact, during the just over half an hour drive sitting in the backseat of the midnight-black Lincoln Town Car—Floyd had insisted that Chase sit in the back, even though she felt uncomfortable with being driven around—Chase learned more than she would watching an hour of *Cosmos*.

The first thing that she learned was that Floyd liked to talk. A lot.

Part of this, Floyd explained, was that his speech therapist had told him that getting over the psychological block of speaking would help improve his stutter.

Chase wasn't so sure.

Floyd Montgomery was twenty-four years old and was the nephew of Girdwood's Chief of Police. He had worked for his uncle and the local PD doing odd jobs since he was just a kid, had a sister who had moved to Montreal when she was seven with her dad, neither of whom Floyd ever saw, and he had a keen interest in trains.

A *real* keen interest.

Chase listened as the man spoke, mostly out of politeness rather than interest, and when Floyd finally paused to take a breath, she broke in.

"So, Floyd, any idea where, exactly, we're going?" she asked, watching as the subdued metropolis of Anchorage, which was centered around the airport, began to thin into a white expanse.

Floyd's eyes flicked up to the rearview, before quickly returning to the road.

"Yes; Girdwood, small t-t-town about forty minutes f-from Anchorage. Well, t-t-technically we're going to Crow C-C-Creek Road. Say, this is the first time that I've d-d-driven an FBI agent around. I was pretty excited when Unc—" that's what he called the Police Chief, *Unc*, as if he were eight and not three times that age, "—said that I'd be chaperoning not one, but, t-t-two FBI Agents. I mean, that's p-p-pretty exciting, don't you think?"

Again, his pale eyes flicked up.

The question seemed rhetorical to Chase, but concerned that his eyes remained locked on hers and not the road for so long, she eventually offered an answer.

"Well, I bet you're pretty disappointed, huh?" she said with a wry smile. Despite his ramblings, after everyone that she had encountered today, Floyd was a breath of fresh air.

He turned his eyes back to the road.

"W-w-well, I don't know about t-t-that. You're very p-p-pretty."

For some reason, Floyd's innocence struck a chord with her and Chase started to blush. Turning her gaze to the dark, tinted windows, she stared at her own reflection.

Seeing the dark circles under her eyes, her hair that she had been forced to pull back in a short ponytail after falling asleep between the two giants on the plane, she thought briefly that Floyd was messing with her.

But something told her that this simple man wasn't capable of being dishonest.

"Thank you," she said, watching as the landscape further degenerated into a sea of white.

The next five minutes passed in silence, but then they drove over a set of train tracks, and this set Floyd off on a tangent on his favorite subject.

"In 1909, Alaska Central Railroad—th-th-that's the company name—built the f-f-first railroad in Alaska. It was f-f-fifty-one miles long, and took food and people to T-T-T-urnagain Arm."

Chase nodded. This seemed to fuel Floyd's excitement, and when he spoke again, his stutter became more pronounced.

"F-f-from there, the d-d-dogs would take the p-p-people and f-food where it needed to g-g-go."

Chase's ears perked.

"Dogs?"

Floyd nodded.

"D-d-dogsleds. I had a dog once," Floyd continued, "His name was S-S-Steven. He w-w-was a co-co-cocker-spaniel. But he died."

Another pause, this one extending as long as a full minute.

"We're almost here," Floyd announced, pulling Chase out of her head.

They had moved from a main highway artery to a feeder capillary, and the metropolis that was Anchorage had become a distant memory. They passed a sign announcing that they were entering Girdwood, then continued through the lazy resort town, before exiting on the other side. In the distance, she could make out snow-covered pines, as well as a narrowing of the road. Floyd turned onto an even smaller road, which Chase assumed, but couldn't tell for certain given the snow, was unpaved.

In the back of her mind, she had expected to see dozens of police cars, an ambulance, maybe, and a Crime Scene Unit on scene, or in the very least, some pomp and circumstance that warranted FBI involvement. But as Floyd brought the car to a slow, she saw nothing but more snow and trees.

Eventually, the familiar shadows of two vehicles jutted from the horizon. One, a Girdwood PD cruiser, lights off, and a dark-colored, unmarked vehicle.

She instinctively knew that the latter belonged to FBI Agent Martinez, who Floyd had mentioned back at the airport, and while she was excited to meet the man who had called her up in the early morning hours, she was disappointed that her first assignment didn't have her paired with Agent Stitts. Still, as they approached the scene, most of her mind was occupied with running scenarios of what she was about to see.

The snow, the remoteness of the location.

The number of roads in, roads out. The one cop car at the scene.

Why call in the FBI? Why not get Anchorage PD out here?

Chase wouldn't have to wait long to have at least some of her questions answered, it appeared, as Floyd parked behind the unmarked car and quickly hopped out.

She reached for the handle, but Floyd had already opened the door for her.

"I'll get it," he said.

The cold was biting, and it shocked the last vestiges of drowsiness from her system. It had been a long, trying day already, but now that she was on scene, Chase felt her adrenaline start to flow.

Pulling the front of her suit jacket tight, she felt ridiculous, and knew that she must look even more absurd than she felt stepping out into the snow in Jimmy Choos without a proper coat. Her only saving grace was the fact that the sun shone brightly overhead, offering some solace from the biting wind.

What a first impression, she thought glumly.

No sooner had she taken three steps into the snow, did two men approach. In the lead was a man in a black parka, large, aviator-style sunglasses that weren't that much unlike her own pair—which had been conveniently packed in her suitcase—and perfect posture. He was of medium height and build, and looked to be in his mid-forties, with tanned skin, and dark hair parted on one side. A frown was etched on his otherwise handsome face.

Behind him was Floyd's uncle, Girdwood's Chief of Police. Unlike Agent Martinez, he was tall and had a thick gut that hung over the belt of his beige pants. The wind wreaked havoc on his thinning hair, but despite these differences, he had a striking resemblance to her driver.

Agent Martinez gave her a once-over as he approached.

"Lost your luggage?" he said with a grin as he neared. "Not the best first impression, huh?"

Chase raised an eyebrow, unsure if the man was referring to her appearance or her impression of Anchorage.

She decided it didn't matter and held out her hand.

"Chase Adams."

"Special Agent Chris Martinez," was the reply. Martinez shook her hand hard, then moved to one side. "And this is Frank Downs, Girdwood Chief of Police."

The burly man strode forward, a smirk on his face.

They shook hands.

"Not this cold in New York, is it?"

"Sixty-eight and cloudy," Chase replied.

"I've got an extra coat in the car," Martinez offered. "You're going to need it."

Chapter 6

Despite their differences in stature—Agent Martinez was at least six inches taller and sixty pounds heavier than her—his spare jacket, a red, down-filled parka, fit Chase fairly well. She put it on, and immediately felt her body start to warm. Her eyes fell on the black box in the trunk, and she was about to say something, when Martinez took the words right out of her mouth.

"Let me guess: your service pistol was also lost?"

Chase nodded.

"They forced me to check it."

Martinez reached for the box and handed it to Chase.

"You can borrow my spare," he said. Chase opened the clasp and peered inside. A midnight-black Glock 22 sat embedded in foam. She took it out, quickly checked the magazine, then reached beneath the coat and slid it into the holster on her hip. That, at least, hadn't been checked.

Martinez stared at her for a moment.

"No-nonsense. I like that."

Chase nodded, then looked around.

Floyd had parked at the side of the road, maybe thirty yards from the edge of a heavily wooded area. As far as she could see in either direction, there were no houses or cabins and, thankfully, no dogs or dogsleds.

"Come with me," Martinez instructed, walking away from the parked vehicles. Chase followed him down a small embankment to a spot that had been disturbed by the snow.

"This is where the bodies were found: two girls, both sophomores at University of Alaska, Anchorage," Martinez said in a voice reminiscent of someone reading a script. "Yolanda Strand and Francine Butler. Both girls were found here yesterday by a trucker shipping goods north to the Valdez-Cordova region. Immediately called it in."

Chase stared at the two indentations in the snow. The area was much larger than should have been made by just two bodies, and she assumed that the rest of the disruption must have been made either by the trucker or CSU.

"Where are the bodies now?"

"At the morgue," the Police Chief answered. "Been there since yesterday."

"And the trucker?"

"Well known in the neighborhood. His name is Henry Buckley, but everyone around here calls him Big Rig."

"And the girls? How did they get here?"

Martinez shook his head.

"Don't know—went missing two days ago. Their bodies were discovered before anyone actually reported them missing—they were rooming at the university and when they didn't show up to class, it was assumed that they had partied too hard the night before. Both had just written their final exam for…" Martinez paused as he thought about this for a moment, "… Eastern Philosophy, I believe."

Chase continued to look around as Martinez spoke. Aside from the indentations in the snow, there was nothing else out of the ordinary, so far as she could tell, in this foreign landscape.

"I brought you out here to get a scope of the scene, of the lay of the land. I wanted you to see how secluded the area was."

Chase nodded, and found her eyes returning to the forest. She was reminded of the two girls that she had found in the barn in Larchmont County, the ones with the lips painted in blood, and the forest that extended from the rear of the barn.

"Frank and his men have already searched most of the forest," Martinez said, following her gaze. "Didn't come up with anything useful."

"Two college-aged girls…" Chase muttered, partly to herself, "How were they killed? Any evidence of sexual assault?"

Martinez shook his head.

"Not as far as we can tell. Things move a little more slowly here than you might be used to in NYC. These two murders were the first in Girdwood in over fifteen years."

Chase lifted an eyebrow, but it was Chief Downs who continued.

"Two homicides occurred on a reservation, and before that there were only three others on record. Those are thought to be drug-related." Downs had a hard expression on his face as he spoke, and Chase got the impression that he was none too happy that these were still unsolved, despite the fact that, given his age, it was unlikely he was in charge when they had taken place.

"How were the girls killed?" Chase asked again.

Chief Downs shifted uncomfortably, his thick boots crunching snow beneath his heels.

"Exposure and blood loss," Martinez said.

Chase thought of her own outfit, prior to taking Martinez up on the offer of using his extra parka. It *was* cold out, but not so cold that she wouldn't have been able to make the trek back to Girdwood. She would be frost-bitten, surely, but wouldn't die from exposure, she didn't think.

"Why didn't—"

"Their feet were cut off," Chief Downs said, a far off look in his eyes.

Chase blinked.

"What?"

Downs turned to face her then, and she saw that it wasn't just the fact that murders were unsolved that bothered him, but he took this personally. She had the sudden impression that the large man took everything that happened in Girdwood and the surrounding areas personally.

"The two girls were naked, and their feet were severed. Best we can figure it, this is a secondary location. Their feet were removed elsewhere, and they were dropped here," Downs extended his finger beyond the disturbed snow. "We think that this is where they were dropped, but managed to make their way to here."

Chase's mind started to whir.

Made their way? Without feet?

"How do you know?"

The Chief's expression grew stern.

"That's where their clothes were found."

Chase swallowed hard.

And this is why the FBI was brought in, she thought, not with pride, but with something akin to disgust.

And yet, despite these disturbing facts, they weren't the only thing that struck her as odd.

"Where's the blood?" she asked. "If their feet were removed... where's all the blood?"

Chief Downs's frown became a scowl.

"That's the thing, Agent Adams... there isn't any."

Chapter 7

"**It's called paradoxical undressing,**" the Medical Examiner told them. Girdwood didn't have its own morgue, so after observing the scene, Chase, Agent Martinez, and Chief Downs had made the trek back to Anchorage.

The ME was a thin, wiry creature that pretty much filled every cliché of a doctor who was squirreled away in a hospital basement: small, beady eyes, a twitching nose, bald head covered in freckles. When he spoke, the words came out in a flurry as if he so infrequently came into contact with other humans that he was worried he had forgotten how to formulate a complete sentence.

"Pardon?" Chase asked as she observed the bodies. Lying side-by-side on metal gurneys were the two victims. Yolanda Strand was African-American, with hair pulled back in corn rows. Francine Butler, on the other hand, was pale, but judging by the white patches forming the familiar outline of a bathing suit on her pubic region and covering her small breasts, she had clearly made efforts to try to change that.

The ME sighed as if this conversation was boring him, which it probably was.

"Paradoxical undressing: when a person is close to freezing, they suddenly feel warm and take off all their clothes."

Chase took this in stride, her eyes drifting down the bodies.

Both girls were in fairly good shape, and other than the pallor of their skin, they looked relatively healthy.

"It happens in—" the doctor continued, but Chase held up a finger, stopping him mid-sentence. She could sense Chief Downs and Agent Martinez staring at her, likely with eyebrows raised, but she didn't lift her gaze from the corpses.

Her breathing suddenly slowed, and she allowed her eyes to defocus, the bodies of the two girls merging as one, cocoa-colored amalgamation.

Use your gut, Chase. Millions of years of evolution have made your body sensitive to cues that your conscious mind is too preoccupied to notice. Allow your mind to drift. Reverse engineer the crime.

Agent Jeremy Stitts's words flowed through her mind, not like an echo, but like a leaf carried in a slow-moving stream.

Her hand suddenly slipped from her side and grazed Yolanda's still-frozen shin.

Let the cues wash over you, put yourself in the victim's shoes.

"Let us go... please. We haven't done anything to you," Yolanda spat. Her lips were trembling, her hands shaking. She glanced over at Francine, but her friend had tucked her head between her knees and hadn't spoken for some time.

"I'll... I'll do anything you want," Yolanda said, her voice changing, becoming softer. She reached out with her hands, which were bound at the wrists, and brushed a finger against the man's calf. His back was to her, and he was crouched, rooting through something in a bag just out of sight. The van was still running, and the heat was on, but Yolanda could see the snow starting to pick up outside.

Dressed only in a thin dress, she knew that she wouldn't last long out there if their captor decided to release them.

The strange smell in the van, like the scent of a stove after someone had just finished deep-frying chicken wings, made her think, however, that this might be the least of her worries.

"Please."

Her fingers teased at the fabric of his pants, and he turned.

And then he started to laugh.

"Anything," she pleaded. "I'll do anything as long as you let us go."

The man moved something into view then, something that gleamed brightly under the van's dome light.

"You beg just like she did—like she pleaded for someone to help, to free her."

Yolanda's eyes widened as confusion washed over her.

"Oh, I'll let you go alright. But I don't think you'll get very far."

It was only then that Yolanda realized the gleam was from a handsaw, and she started to scream.

Chase stumbled, the dizzy spell that hit her so strong that she felt close to vomiting. Her hands splayed out in front of her, and thankfully the gurney on which Yolanda's corpse lay caught her fall.

"Chase? You okay?" a voice asked, but it seemed so far away that she failed to recognize it.

Chase breathed deeply in through her nose and closed her eyes, trying to fight the spins. She wasn't sure what had happened, but it felt for a moment as if *she* were Yolanda, like Chase had somehow been transported inside the woman's head just before the killer—

A hand fell on her back.

"Get her some water! Doc, get her some water!" she heard Martinez say. "Go!"

Chase straightened, and opened her eyes. With one final breath, she felt the last of the nausea pass.

"I'm okay," she said dryly.

Martinez's grip on her tightened.

"You sure? What happened?"

Chase's eyes began to focus again, and she found herself staring at Yolanda's wrists. Even though the skin was frozen, she thought she could make out the faintest pattern from a braided rope.

Did I see this before when I was looking at the bodies, but it didn't register?

Chase was still confused as to what had happened—one minute she was recalling Agent Stitts's words about instinct and gut feelings, the next she was bound and frightened—but tried to recall what she had seen before it was forgotten.

They were in a van... a cargo van.

She turned to Martinez.

"Were there... tire tracks at the scene?" she asked. Martinez finally relinquished his grip on her shoulders and took a step backward. One of his eyebrows twitched slightly.

"Yes... the truck driver who pulled over to the side of the road."

Chase shook her head.

"No, not that big. Something smaller, but bigger than a car..." She tried to think back to the indentations at the scene. Had she seen tire tracks there? From a cargo van? Or had she just made that up?

The entire vision had been so vivid, so pristine, that just thinking about it threatened to make her ill again.

"I'm not sure," Martinez said at last. "We took some casts of whatever we could find at the scene, but with the snow... I don't think there's anything usable. I'll put a call in, however. You—you sure you're okay, Chase?"

Chase ignored the last part, and turned her attention back to Yolanda.

Her eyes moved from her wrists, to her painted fingernails, then down the exterior to the thighs.

The legs ended too soon: the feet were gone, replaced by a scarred and blackened mess where they should have been.

The killer had cauterized the wounds, she realized.

Chase suddenly shook her head, remembering the question that she had asked at the scene.

"The killer didn't sexually assault them," she said in a quiet voice. "But he did watch them... he watched them suffer."

Chapter 8

"So, you gonna tell me what the hell that was all about?" Martinez asked, finally breaking the ice.

Chase was having a hard time reading the man. She thought that she had a good idea of who Agent Jeremy Stitts was, what made him *tick*, what made him *tock*, but with Martinez? He was elusive, holding his cards close to his chest. In fact, if it hadn't been for her rather candid interactions with Stitts, she would have expected that Martinez was the prototypical FBI Agent.

But Stitts had broken that mold, and now nothing seemed to fit.

Guided by her vision, or whatever the hell the episode Chase had was, Martinez had sent another CSU crew out to Girdwood to see if they could gather any evidence of the presence of a large van. Although Chase was skeptical that they could have combed the entire scene during the day, day and a half, between when the bodies had been discovered and she had arrived, Martinez cautioned her not to mention her apprehension to Chief Downs. The man was sensitive to anything that might be considered a slight on either him or his department. Right now, their relationship was amicable, and Chief Downs's limited experience with these types of murders made it clear that they needed the FBI's help. Agent Martinez, who clearly had a long-standing relationship with the man, was the one who floated the idea that CSU return to the scene to look for evidence of a van.

Chief Downs had reluctantly agreed, but not without muttering something derogatory about 'clairvoyance.' Still, despite his grumblings, he had ordered a crew back out to the scene.

"I don't know," Chase said at last. "It's never... it's never happened to me before. It was like..."

She let her sentence trail off as she searched for the right words.

What had it been like?

Truthfully, it had felt like she, Chase Edith Adams, 32 years old, had become Yolanda Strand, 22 years old.

Like she had been *her*.

It had also felt like the first time she injected heroin. It had been an out-of-body experience, it had been disorienting, and it had made her feel sick when she finally came down.

But, of course, this latter part wasn't something she could share with Martinez.

She looked across the table at the man, who sat, beer poised but not quite touching his lips.

He wanted an answer, so Chase gave him one.

"It was like reading a book," was the best she could come up with—the most benign analogy her tired brain could generate. "Reading a really good book."

It was obtuse, but Martinez seemed to accept her answer, and finally took a sip of his beer.

"Not hungry?" he asked after swallowing. His dark eyes flicked to the plate of food that lay in front of her.

Chase had ordered a club sandwich on brown bread— trying to be healthy after the greasy mess of a burger she had devoured at lunch—and a green salad, but the wilted lettuce leaves, which appeared to have been scraped from a picky patron's burger, made her stomach churn.

She still hadn't completely recovered from her... *vision*.

"Just tired," she said. "It's been a long day."

Martinez nodded, jammed some fries into his mouth, and chased them with another sip of beer.

"I hear you."

Except Martinez didn't look tired in the least.

"How about you?"

He shrugged.

"I'm alright. Arrived four days ago. More than enough time to acclimate."

Chase raised an eyebrow. Four days ago was before the murders had been committed. Martinez must have recognized something on her face, as he said, "Was here on other business. Me and the Chief have... history."

The way he said the word *history* made it clear that he wasn't keen on discussing it further.

Which was fine by Chase. Everyone had their secrets, including her, and save sitting around in a circle with incense burning and singing Kumbaya, she intended on keeping it this way.

"Listen, I got you set up at a motel not ten minutes from here. It's nothing special—" Martinez laughed, "—but it should do the trick. I've got a room just a few doors down."

He produced a key with a ridiculously large dongle that had the number 17 engraved on one side.

Chase took it from his hand.

"Thanks," she said, to which Martinez nodded.

"Just let me finish up here, and then we'll get going. Tired or not, I need to sleep. It's going to be a long day tomorrow."

Chapter 9

'NOTHING SPECIAL' TURNED OUT to be one of the most ridiculous understatements that Chase had ever heard.

Girdwood Motel looked on the verge of being condemned. Chase's experience on her flight had dissolved any illusions of private jets and champagne, but this? This was too much.

Or too little, as it were.

"Does the trick," Martinez said as he pulled the rental into the empty lot. There was a hint of defensiveness in the man's voice, something that suggested that he had stayed here before.

Why that would be the case, Chase had absolutely no clue.

"Hey, what's with the kid, Floyd?" she asked before they exited the vehicle.

Martinez turned off the car and turned to face her.

"What do you mean?"

Chase shrugged. She wasn't exactly sure *what* she meant, anymore than she knew what had happened to her in the morgue. Still, she felt compelled to open a dialog about the man.

"Is he really the Chief's nephew?"

Although her experience at the morgue had set her mind into a frenzy, she had actively pushed these thoughts into deeper faculties, not wanting to bias herself by creating a profile before she had all the facts. And yet something about Floyd had struck her as… *off*. And it wasn't just the fact that he was a little slow.

After all, a man with a stutter, of a similar age to the victims… it wouldn't be the first time that someone had gone off the deep end and extracted revenge for incessant bullying.

"Huh. I'm not sure. He calls Chief Downs his uncle, and they sure as hell look alike, but the Chief hasn't directly told me that they're related. He's always just hanging around… for as long as I've known the Chief, Floyd has been in the picture." Martinez paused. "Why? You getting a vibe?"

Chase hesitated before replying.

"No, not really. Just curious. Is he going to drive me again tomorrow?"

"If you want. I'm a notorious early riser, and I can see that you need some rest. If I'm gone before you wake, I'll have him swing by."

"And he'll be alright with that?"

Martinez laughed.

"Alright? The guy thinks he's some sort of driver for the president. The boy's in heaven."

Chase nodded, thinking about how nervous the man had been when he had first approached her in the airport.

"What's the plan for tomorrow, anyway?"

Martinez's hand hovered over the door handle, and Chase suddenly felt foolish—no, not foolish, but *amateurish* for asking such a question.

"I thought you'd want to speak to the truck driver who found the bodies."

"Yes, of course," Chase said quickly, trying to recover. "And then maybe we can talk to some of Yolanda and Francine's friends at the university."

"Sounds like a plan," Martinez replied as he stepped out into the cold.

They walked in silence toward the rows of rooms, half of which were missing either part or all of the numbers indicating which room they actually were.

Martinez stopped in front of a door with a one—the second number had long since either rotted away or had been stolen—his key poised by the lock.

"This is me," he said without turning. "Yours is three down. Get some rest, Adams, and I'll see you in the morning."

Chase said goodnight and continued down the row of rooms. She identified number 17 not by the digits on the door, it was, in fact, missing both number, but because it was sandwiched between 1— and 18. She tried her key and the door opened.

To her surprise, the interior of the small motel room was in considerably better shape than the exterior. Still no *Four Seasons*, she realized that what Martinez had said had some ring of truth to it.

Nothing special.

And yet it would do the trick.

She checked the glowing numbers on the clock beside the bed.

It was five minutes to nine, which meant in NYC time, it was almost one in the morning.

Her first inclination was to shower, to scrape the residue of the day from her skin, but when she sat on the quilted mattress to remove her Choos, it was clear that she wasn't going to make it that far.

I'll just rest for a minute or two, she thought, knowing that these were famous last words even as they formulated in her mind.

Sleep took her like the moon takes night.

"Chase? Chase? Please, you need to help me."
Georgina's words were haunting, desperate.

"Tell me where you are," Chase whispered into the dark. "Please, Georgie, just tell me where you are."

Chase was somewhere cold and damp, the walls slick with condensation. She tried to look around, but everything seemed to blur as if she were moving extremely fast instead of rooted in place.

"Chase? Are you there?"

She felt her heart rate quicken.

"I'm here, Georgie. I'm here, just tell me where you are, and I'll come get you."

Chase's voice sounded like her own, like her 32-year-old self, but when Georgina replied, she did so in the same voice as the day she had been abducted: that of a five-year-old girl, hot, nervous, and afraid.

My god, she seemed terrified.

"Why did you run, Chase? Why didn't you stay? We could have gotten away together."

Chase felt her chest hitch.

"I wanted to… I wanted to stay, but he would have grabbed us both. I had—" no choice, *she tried to say, but her throat was suddenly too constricted to answer.*

It was a lie. She had had a choice, and her decision was to run. But she was only seven, and although she was two years Georgina's elder, she too was just a child.

"I—I—"

The shadows in front of her, previously impenetrable, suddenly started to pixelate.

And then Chase saw her sister as she had been that day. Her blond hair damp with sweat, her eyes wide, her face glistening in whatever dream lights existed in this place.

Strangely, she was crawling.

Chase tried to stand, but her body was frozen in place. When Georgina continued to crawl toward her, fear suddenly struck Chase, and instead of wanting to go to her sister, she suddenly felt a strong urge to run in the opposite direction.

Just as she had that summer day.

"Please," she moaned. "Please, Georgina. I'm sorry..."

Georgina continued toward her, eyes wide, mouth twisted in a grimace of exertion.

When she was nearly on top of Chase, she suddenly turned back.

"My legs... there's something wrong with my legs..." the girl whispered.

Chase followed her sister's gaze, then she started to scream.

Chapter 10

Sleep vacated Chase Adams nearly as quickly as it had come.

She was awake when Martinez's door opened, and watched as he made his way toward his car, breathing large puffs of warm air into cupped hands to warm them.

He didn't turn to look at her, didn't so much as glance in the direction of Room 17.

He's letting me sleep, she thought.

But Chase couldn't sleep, not after the harrowing nightmare of seeing her sister relieved of her feet.

And yet Chase didn't open the door. In fact, after Martinez started his car, she closed the cheap plastic blinds completely.

There was something about Floyd, something that didn't seem right to her. And she relished the opportunity to speak to him again.

A glance at the clock indicated that it wasn't quite six yet, local time. Chase had been awake since one, only catnapping from then until now, and was still feeling the effects of jet lag and fatigue.

Still, after a warm shower, Chase found that most of the exhaustion sluiced off her. After dabbing cover-up beneath her eyes, and on the inside of her elbows to hide the scars, she moved to the bed… and realized that the only clothes she had were the ones that she had worn all day yesterday.

"Shit," she grumbled. Wrapping the towel, which had a thread count of about seven, around her waist, Chase reached for her cell phone.

She turned it on, and her frown became intractable. There were no missed calls, no texts waiting. The airline was one thing, but Brad? Brad and Felix?

It had been a few days since she had spoken to either of them, and it wasn't like them not to check in, especially given the messages she had left. But rather than call her family, she dialed the number scrawled on the back of the luggage ticket instead.

Now close to seven, she was surprised when it was answered on the first ring. What didn't impress her, however, was that she was fairly certain it was the same man she had spoken to the day before. The one with the temperament of a sedated goat.

"Hi," Chase said, trying not to let exasperation creep into her voice. "I'm calling about my luggage... it never made it to Anchorage from Seattle."

"Can I have your name and ticket number, please."

Chase's eyes darted to the luggage tag.

"Chase Adams, number 101A434."

"Please hold."

Before she could say anything, the line clicked, and she was acquainted with the sound of a tuba playing at the end of a long hallway.

Movement in her periphery caught her eye, and Chase looked toward the window. Even though she had closed the blinds after Martinez had left, they were bent in several places and she could still see into the parking lot. A black Lincoln Town Car appeared, slowed, and then stopped outside her door.

The line clicked.

"Mrs. Adams?"

"Yes? Has my stuff arrived?"

"I don't think so."

"What? What do you mean, *you don't think so?* It's either there, or it isn't."

"Well there are several bags without tags. Can you please describe your bag to me?"

Chase sighed and closed her eyes, recalling the image of her suitcase.

"It's a plain black suitcase, has ADAMS written on the tag."

"Is that all?"

Chase opened her eyes and shook her head.

What else do you need?

"Yes, that's all."

"One moment, please."

The tuba returned, and Chase had to breathe through her mouth and nose to retain control.

Eventually, just as the driver-side door of the Lincoln Town Car started to open, the man returned.

"No, I'm sorry, but there is no luggage that meets your description."

"Fine," Chase snapped. "I have an address now, if you could be so kind as to take that down?"

"Mm-hmm, go ahead."

Chase gave the man *Girdwood Motel's* address from a book of matches on the bedside table, and told him that she was in Room 17.

"Okay, we'll be in touch as soon as—"

Chase hung up the phone, and, almost as if he had been waiting for this moment, Floyd knocked on the door.

"A-A-Agent Adams? It's Floyd. Agent M-M-Martinez said to come by and p-p-pick you up."

Chase begrudgingly started to dress in the same clothes as yesterday.

"I'll be right out," she said.

"O-Okay, I'll w-w-wait in the car," Floyd replied.

She saw him walk, hunched, to his car and get back into the driver seat.

After dressing and trying her best to smooth out the wrinkles on her white blouse, Chase took the pistol still in the holster and strapped it around her waist. Next, she pulled the red parka on, and zipped it up tight.

Out of habit, she turned back to the room before she stepped out into the cold, to see if she had left anything behind, before realizing that she had nothing *to* leave behind.

With a frown, she opened the door and stepped outside.

Chase immediately turned her eyes upward. The sun shone brightly in the sky, and it must have been a good twenty degrees warmer than yesterday. The dark clouds that had formed on their drive from the crime scene to Alaska Regional Hospital had since disappeared, and it felt more like October in New York than March in Alaska.

Floyd rolled down the window.

"O-O-Over here, Chase," he said with a grin.

Chase couldn't help but return the expression. Floyd's unmistakable Town Car was the only one in the motel parking lot.

"I can see that, Floyd. I can see that."

Chapter 11

"**Welcome, Agent Adams**," **Chief** Downs said when Chase pulled the door to the conference room wide.

She was surprised to see that three of the Chief's men—likely the grand total of Girdwood officers—were already seated at small desks in front of the man, with Martinez standing at his side.

Chase felt her face redden as she made her way toward an open desk.

"So glad that you could finally join us."

Chase kept her head low.

What the hell? Why didn't Martinez tell me that there was a powwow scheduled?

At the greasy spoon the night prior, he had told her the plan was just to interview the driver again.

Shaking her head, Chase pulled a chair out and was about to sit, when Martinez addressed her directly.

"Up here, Agent Adams," he said.

Chase raised her head, and realized that all eyes were on her. If her face had been red before, it had now turned a shade of purple that Oprah would have been proud of.

"Sorry," she grumbled, pushing the chair back into place. She walked to the front of the room, doing her best to keep her head held high this time.

She didn't know if this was some sort of rookie initiation by Agent Martinez, or if he was simply being a dick, but she didn't much care, either.

This petty act reminded her of how the old Sergeant at 62nd precinct NYPD had treated her before she had taken his position.

Do these people not take anything seriously? There are two dead girls sans *feet, in a morgue not a twenty-minute drive from here, and their priority is to embarrass me?*

Chase swallowed hard and ground her teeth.

Maybe it was her stature, the fact that she was a woman, or the fact that she was attractive, or maybe it was all of these things working in concert to ensure that others didn't take her seriously.

Didn't treat her with respect.

"Thank you," Chief Downs said with a sly grin when she had finally taken up residence beside him.

The charade apparently complete, Martinez stepped forward and said, "This is Special Agent Chase Adams, she will be assisting me on this investigation. I ask that you give her your full cooperation."

Chase glared at him.

You want them to show me respect? After what you just pulled?

Chase desperately wanted to say something, to come back with a quip, but bit her tongue.

It had been her dream, her goal to become an FBI Agent, and she wasn't going to jeopardize this on her first case, no matter how unconventional things had been up to this point.

Instead, she locked eyes with any of the Girdwood PD who dared look in her direction.

She had been through this before, of course, and knew that the one thing that these bullies craved more than anything was a response.

And Chase refused to give them one.

"Now that the introductions are done," Downs said, "I'll give you a rundown of what we know to date. As you guys are probably aware, two days ago a truck driver," he used a pointer to tap at a photograph taped to the blackboard behind him, "Henry Buckly found the bodies as he was shipping goods north. The frozen stiffs—" Chase cringed at the term as he moved the pointer to photos of the two girls, "—were Yolanda Strand and Francine Butler, both 22, both sophomores at University of Alaska, Anchorage. Their feet had been hacked off with what CSU thinks is a heavy-duty hacksaw, and then the wounds were crudely cauterized with something very hot." The pointer moved to images of the stumps, and Chase saw several of the men in the audience cringe. "Forensic pathology has confirmed that while it would have been difficult to remove the feet, the cauterizing was extremely crude—our unsub likely has some, but not extensive, medical knowledge. Or a good internet connection, I suppose. Agent Martinez?"

Martinez strode forward.

"Based on the age and sex of the victims, historical statistics indicate that we are looking for a male between the ages of twenty-five and forty. Officer Mills already spoke to the victims' friends at the university, none of whom reported Yolanda nor Francine as missing—two days wasn't out of the question for the girls, especially given that they had gone out partying the day we think they went missing. Several of them saw the victims intoxicated at a local university pub, and the ME has confirmed that both had high, but tolerable levels of alcohol in their systems. Francine had low levels of cocaine in her system, but the ME has ruled out that they were drugged," he paused. It seemed too early to Chase to formulate a profile; there was just too much they didn't know, but Martinez had no reservations it appeared. "Look, I know what you're thinking: these girls might have gone with anyone, given how rare violence of this nature is in Anchorage. But this isn't nineteen eighty-five—ignorance is a thing of the past. These girls, no matter how drunk, would have their radar going if they were approached by anyone suspicious, isn't that right, Chase?"

Chase didn't immediately hear her name, and continued to stare.

"Chase?" Martinez asked, raising an eyebrow. "Don't you think that these girls would be on alert if approached by someone... a man... who seemed *off*?"

Chase blinked and shook her head lightly.

Her face threatened to blush again, but she forced it away. A quick glance confirmed that she was the only woman in the room, and the words of the greasy TSA agent sounded in her head.

Bitches... you told the women of New York to act like bitches to avoid being targeted.

"Maybe," she said at last. "Given that there were two of them, they were likely using the buddy system at the bar, something that is common among young females who are planning a night of drinking."

Martinez stared at her for a moment before turning back to Girdwood PD. Several of the men were smirking, Chase noted.

A big part of her wanted to ask what the fuck was so humorous to demand it, and she would have—she would have told them all off—except this was all new to her and, having wanted to be an FBI Agent for as long as she could remember, stayed her tongue.

All of it felt somewhat surreal and not that much unlike what had happened in the morgue yesterday.

"I'll take that as a yes, which means that the person who approached them was likely of average or of better than average looks, someone who would fit in the university bar scene. I think we should focus on—"

"—or our killer could have been a person of authority, a doctor, maybe, but probably not based on the forensic report, or a police officer, teacher, that sort of thing," Chase offered.

She was thinking about her last case, about how FBI Agent Stitts had developed a profile of a man similar to the one that Martinez was describing now, and it had blinded them.

The real killer had been a woman.

Chase was thinking of this, and not about the words that were coming out of her mouth.

Martinez's lips twisted into a scowl, and Chase immediately regretted speaking up. She was, after all, *assisting* him in the investigation, not leading it. And yet the selfish part of her was glad that he was now the one who felt uncomfortable.

A strained silence fell over the group as Martinez glared at her, but she refused to look away.

Her thoughts turned to Yolanda and Francine, of them in the van, desperate, crying, knowing that these moments would likely be their last on Earth.

"Any questions? Comments?" Chief Downs eventually asked.

A man with a thin mustache raised his hand.

"What about the truck driver? Is he a suspect?"

Chief Downs shook his head.

"Not at this time. Agents Martinez and Adams will further vet him later today, but for now it looks like he just came across the bodies."

"The killer probably drove a van," Chase interjected, "a cargo van, maybe, something large enough to house the girls, and bound them with rope. His motives are unknown, but the fact that he cut their feet off and watched them suffer, watched them try to crawl out of the cold, indicates that the killer might be hung up on the idea of a woman running away from him. A mother abandoning him at birth, or something even less substantial; a wife who left him, a girlfriend who scorned him. I will stress, however, that none of what either myself or Agent Martinez are saying is fact. We are trying to guide you, give you something to look out for, but not something that you should focus on specifically."

Chief Downs nodded and then turned to his men.

"I want you guys to make your presence known in the university. Set up shop, ask questions. There might be something there that links these girls to the killer. As always, eyes and ears open, people."

He paused, and when no one moved, he gestured dramatically with his hands.

"Dismissed! Go!"

The men leapt to their feet, their chairs scraping noisily across the floor. The sound was unexpectedly grating to Chase and she winced. Whenever she suffered from a lack of sleep, which was often these days and even more so since Brad and Felix left, loud sounds seemed like a pickaxe in her brain.

She was so focused on blocking out the sound, that she didn't even hear Agent Martinez approach.

"Don't ever do that again," he hissed.

Chase turned and was about to say something, but Martinez was already heading toward the door.

"What about the trucker? Aren't we going to—"

"Get Floyd to take you," Martinez spat over his shoulder. "Stitts said you were a team player, now it's time to get with the program, Adams."

Chapter 12

THE TRUCKER'S NAME WAS Henry T. Buckly; he was forty-six, overweight, and had a dark beard that was thicker on his throat than on his chin. And yet, despite his gruff appearance, all indications were that he was a soft-spoken man who was genuinely shocked and affected by finding the two girls in the empty field by the side of the road.

"Mr. Buckly, can you please go over what you were doing in the time leading up to your discovery of the bodies?" Agent Martinez asked.

The man's dark eyes darted across the table to Agent Martinez, then to Chase who sat beside her partner. His eyes softened when their gaze met, and she knew that he was ashamed by what he had seen.

By their naked bodies.

"Why?" he said quietly. "I already told you everything I saw."

Agent Martinez cleared his throat.

"Mr. Buckly—"

"Why do you keep calling me that? My name's Henry—call me Henry for Christ's sake."

The man's eyes darted over to Chase again, and she opened her mouth to say something—she knew that all she had to do is be polite with Henry, to gently ask him to tell the story once more, just one more time for her benefit, and he would come right out with it—but she saw a muscle in Agent Martinez's dark hairline tense and knew that he was grinding his teeth.

After the scolding the man had given her at the station for speaking up about the preliminary profile, Chase was hesitant to cross him again.

Her mind flicked to the Download Killer, the fact that it was a woman all along, and the profile had called for a man.

But if it means...

"Fine, *Henry*—tell me once more what happened," Martinez snapped.

Henry took a deep breath, and his large gut, hidden behind a Def Leppard T-shirt, rose and fell.

He lowered his gaze and began to speak.

"I was doing my regular route—Anchorage to Valdez-Cordova—and I knew a shortcut that I could—"

"Have you taken this shortcut before?" Martinez demanded.

Chase looked over at him. While Martinez may have heard the story before, several times it seemed, Chase hadn't, and she wanted to hear it without interruptions.

"Yeah, like I told you, I always take the smaller roads as I exit the city, then reconnect with the main artery about fifty miles out. Takes an hour off my trip and saves gas."

"Does your supervisor know about this? Dispatch? Is it common?"

Henry squirmed in his seat.

"No, I mean, I guess they do now. It's not something that they recommend, because if something goes wrong with the rig, insurance might have a problem with it. But everyone does it. I've done it for my last seven trips without any issues. I mean, I have two young daughters, and if it means I can have two extra hours with them after a round trip? Then, yeah, I bend the rules a little. But so what? I'm just—"

Martinez leaned back in his chair.

"Go on. Tell me what happened after you took your shortcut."

Me... not us, tell me.

Chase was getting frustrated with Agent Martinez's machismo, or ego, or whatever it was. Sure, this was her first case, but how was she supposed to help if he treated her like she wasn't even there?

"Okay, well, I was taking the route I told you already, and then I saw the bodies at the side of the road—"

"Well, here's the thing, Henry, this is the part of the story I'm having a hard time understanding. I get the shortcut, fine, we've already spoken to several of your colleagues, and after some pressing they've also admitted to taking that route." Martinez leaned forward. "You know how many other drivers took that same road the day you found the girls?"

Henry shook his head. His eyes were darting now, only they weren't landing on anything in particular. Chase knew this face. This was the face of a rabbit caught in the snare, of a man who was about to lawyer up.

"No idea," he said at last. Quiet before, Henry was nearly inaudible now.

"Three. Three drivers drove right by the women, and didn't stop. I mean, it must have been hard to see them, right? Half-covered in snow, at least fifty feet from the road. Not only that, but there were flurries at the time, weren't there?"

Henry looked to Chase for support, but before she could say or do anything, Martinez snapped his fingers, drawing the trucker's gaze back.

"Not a rhetorical question, Henry. It was snowing out, wasn't it?"

"I don't—I mean, I think it was."

"Yeah, it was. It was snowing like hell. And yet you, driving a goddamn eighteen wheeler loaded with… what exactly were you carrying, Henry?"

Henry's eyes suddenly darkened.

"I think I want a lawyer," he said softly, and Chase felt her chest drop. Ever since entering the room, she knew that they weren't going to get anything from this guy, not with the Armstrong approach, anyway.

Martinez cupped his ear.

"What? I can't hear you... did you say something, Henry?"

Henry stood and slammed his hands down on the table. The movement was so sudden, the noise so loud, that Chase jumped.

"I said, *I want my lawyer!*" he bellowed.

Martinez, who hadn't moved with the outburst, chuckled.

"That's what I thought you said. But you don't need one, Henry."

"I *what?*"

"I said, you don't need one. You're free to go."

Henry blinked but didn't move.

Martinez waved a hand, dismissing the big man.

"Go on, get back to your life. Get out of my face."

When Henry still didn't so much as lean toward the door, Martinez added, "Go now, Henry. Go, before I change my mind and do an inventory of exactly what you were carrying that day."

Henry's eyes widened, but he left the room without another word.

Chase, heart still pounding away in her chest, breathed deeply when he was finally gone.

What the hell was that all about?

Chapter 13

THE DOOR SLAMMED CLOSED and Chase turned to face Agent Martinez. She had been in interrogations with strong men before, including the inimitable Damien Drake, but this was... *what?*

Chase wasn't sure what it was, so she went ahead and asked.

"What the hell was that?"

Martinez shrugged.

"I had to know."

Chase gaped.

"Know what?"

"That he wasn't the one."

Chase felt on thin ice here but couldn't help herself. Martinez's candor was alarming.

"I have no idea what the—"

Martinez turned to face her.

"Agent Stitts warned me about you," he suddenly said. The comment made Chase to recoil.

"What?"

"Stitts said that you liked to see the good in everyone, that you're naive, still a little green, even after everything you've been through."

Chase bit her tongue. She wasn't sure if Martinez was trying to goad her, but these didn't sound like Jeremy Stitts's words. Granted, she hadn't known the man for long, but Chase always pegged herself a good read of character.

And it didn't seem like something Agent Stitts would say.

When she didn't respond, partly because of shock and partly because she refused to be provoked, Martinez interlaced his fingers and leaned toward her.

"Look, I get it. My methods may seem unorthodox to you, but trust me, there's a rhyme to this reason."

This time Chase couldn't restrain herself.

"What? What reason did you have to abuse that man the way you did?"

Martinez chuckled.

"Abused? You've got to be kidding me, Adams. Look, I've been around a lot of cold-blooded murderers in my time, and Henry Buckly? I had to press him. I had to see him break. And he did."

"Yeah, but why that way? Why did—"

"Here's the thing, Chase; I know what cargo he was carrying. Sure, he was bringing produce to Valdez, but he was also shuttling heroin up north. That's why he was so damn cautious out there, why he saw the bodies when none of the other truckers didn't."

This tidbit of information took Chase by surprise. Not necessarily the information itself, but the fact that Agent Martinez was aware of this. Clearly, it hadn't been offered up by Henry himself.

"You knew this, and you let him go?"

Martinez shrugged.

"I'm here to solve these murders, Chase, not shut down a low-level drug smuggler. Besides, he'll get what's coming, scumbags like him always do," Martinez paused, and, for a brief moment, a far-off look fell over his face. Then he shook his head and refocused. "We done here, Chase? Are you done with the grilling? Because if you are, we should probably move on. Henry T. Buckly is clearly not our killer, but one thing's for certain: our guy, whoever the hell he is, isn't done yet. This is only the beginning."

Chase wanted to say more, wanted to question Martinez further, and maybe even prod herself for some answers, but bit her tongue.

She nodded.

"Good," Martinez said as he stood. "CSU called earlier, we should pay them a visit."

***

Chase sat in the backseat of Floyd's Town Car, scratching absently at her arms through the thick jacket.

"You o-o-okay, Agent Adams?" Floyd asked from the front seat.

Chase raised her eyes.

"Hmm?"

"I asked if you were o-okay," he repeated.

"Yeah, I'm fine."

But she didn't sound fine. Even to herself, her voice sounded strained, tired.

Her husband's words echoed in her head.

You're pushing yourself too hard again… remember what happened in Seattle, Chase. Please, take a break. Felix misses you… I miss you.

Chase saw Floyd nodding in the rearview.

"Well if you need anything, you j-j-just let me know."

"Thank you, Floyd."

The drive from the police station to CSU was only about fifteen minutes, and most of that time was passed in silence. But as they approached the building, which was a small, squat structure, emblazoned with a nameplate describing it as *Municipality of Anchorage Crime Scene Investigations*, a thought occurred to her.

"Hey, Floyd?"

"Yes, ma'am?"

"Does your uncle know Agent Martinez?"

"What do you m-m-mean?"

"Before this… have you and Chief Downs met Agent Martinez?" Chase thought she knew the answer already, but just wanted to be sure.

Floyd nodded in the mirror.

"I've met him once before, when I w-w-was younger. B-b-but it was a long time ago. His s-s-sister used to live in Anchorage."

"Hmm."

Before she could press further, Floyd pulled the car up to the front doors, and Chase spotted Agent Martinez standing under a rust-colored awning.

"You want me to w-w-wait?"

Chase looked to Martinez, who was gesturing for her to follow him into CSU.

"I'm not sure," she answered honestly.

"I'll w-w-wait then."

Chase nodded.

"Thanks, Floyd," she said as she stepped out of the car. Tucking her chin into the collar of Martinez's red jacket, she hurried toward the man, worried about what might happen next.

Chapter 14

CHASE FOLLOWED CHIEF DOWNS and Agent Martinez down a long hallway. The men walked with a brisk, determined clip, and her fatigued limbs struggled to keep up.

"They made some additional casts from the area," she overheard the chief tell Martinez. "And there's something that you're going to want to hear for yourself."

Chase picked up the pace.

They entered a small, well-lit room, with a bank of computers on one wall, and what looked to Chase like metal gurneys at the back of the room. She was reminded of Yolanda and Francine's bodies, of how they had been laid out in the morgue, of how she had felt herself transported into the moments before they had been brutalized, stripped, and left out in the cold.

She still hadn't come to grips with what had happened when her hand brushed Yolanda's stump.

"Dr. Trenton, this is FBI Special Agents Martinez and Adams," Chief Downs said, stepping to one side.

Dr. Trenton was a man of average build, with closely cropped black hair, and dark eyes. He stood with his hands jammed into the pockets of his lab coat.

The man pressed his lips together firmly before speaking.

"As I'm sure Chief Downs has told you already, we went back out to the crime scene last night and took some more casts of tire impressions."

He led the way toward one of the gurneys near the back of the room. For some reason, Chase saw Yolanda lying there, her feet ending in scarred and blackened stumps.

She shook her head and the image dissolved into a segment of a cast, a foot and a half long, half as wide. The white plaster was pushed down into a pattern reminiscent of a tire tread.

Which was exactly what it was, of course.

"We found this… tires standard on a 1998 Chevy Cargo Van. I believe it fits the bill of what you were looking for," the man's eyes darted to Chase as he said this last part.

Agent Martinez nodded.

"Chief, see if you can pull up records for all Chevy vans," he shrugged, "between 95 and 99, let's say. Focus on anything local."

Chief Downs agreed but didn't immediately reach for his walkie as Agent Martinez clearly expected. Instead, he said, "Dr. Trenton? That other thing you told me about…?"

Dr. Trenton pressed his lips together again. Chase didn't know if the details of the case were affecting him, or if he was just bored and wanted to get back to a baking soda and vinegar papier-mâché volcano. Tiny vertical creases formed above his lips, making his mouth temporarily look like a puckered anus.

"Yes, please, come with me."

The three of them followed the scientist over to a large computer. Dr. Trenton sat down, and then typed in his username and password when prompted. On screen was a large, close-up image of one of the girl's footless legs.

Please… please, just let us go. We'll do anything…

Dr. Trenton extended a finger toward a particularly gnarled and blackened hunk of flesh.

"See here?" he said.

Chase looked closely, squinted, but didn't see anything other than savagely burned flesh.

Please… anything…

She looked to Chief Downs, who was nodding, but she assumed this was only because Dr. Trenton had already pointed out what he was indicating.

"I don't see anything," Martinez said at last.

"Me neither," Chase agreed.

Dr. Trenton sighed, then grabbed the mouse. A few clicks and the image zoomed in even closer. At this scale, the outer areas started to blur, but there, in the center—

"What's that?" Chase asked, indicating what to her looked like half of a bulls-eye.

Dr. Trenton didn't turn as he answered.

"That's an outline from whatever the killer used to cauterize the wounds."

Chase thought about this for a moment before a fleeting image of a man in khaki pants and a booming voice came to her.

On nights when she didn't play online poker and couldn't sleep either—haunted by what had happened all those years ago and what had happened in Seattle—Chase would lay on the couch, flipping through whatever was on, without really watching anything. And, occasionally, she *would* fall asleep, only to wake up to an infomercial in the wee hours of the morning.

And this was where the shape, a bullseye on the bottom of a pan, seemed familiar.

"It's from a frying pan… the bastard cauterized the wounds with a frying pan."

Even though the words were coming out of her mouth, they sounded foreign to her.

Jesus, a frying pan?

She glanced over at Martinez who was still staring at the spot on the wound, the half bullseye, his head tilted to one side.

"I think you're right," he admitted at last.

Dr. Trenton nodded, and was already two steps ahead of them. He closed the image and opened a browser. A few more clicks, and a photograph of a frying pan appeared onscreen.

"Paderno fryer," he said, his voice strangely reminding Chase of the man in the infomercial. "We've narrowed it down to this one here. It's fairly expensive, just a hair over a hundred bucks at most online retailers."

Now it was Chief Downs's turn to lean in close.

"Is it rare?"

Dr. Trenton shook his head.

"No. Not in the least." He pulled up a map of Anchorage, one that was peppered with small red dots. "Here are the stores that sell this model. More than a hundred in Anchorage alone."

Downs sighed.

"Still, I'll get one of the grunts on it. Tell them to see if they can pull up records of all recent sales of this model."

"There's also online, too," Dr. Trenton continued, "Which are generally fifteen to twenty percent cheaper."

"I'll have them talk to the stores anyway," Downs said, a touch defensively.

A thought occurred to Chase then.

"Hey, Doc, how hot does it have to be to cauterize a wound?"

Dr. Trenton turned to look at her.

"It depends—generally 500 Fahrenheit and up, but in a medical setting it would be done using an electrical current and not heat, *per se*."

"And our vics?" she asked. "What about to cauterize their leg wounds? Can the Paderno cast iron pan get that hot?"

Dr. Trenton pressed his lips together again.

"It's cast iron… it can get very, very hot. To do that to their stumps, though… yeah, I'm guessing it would have to be in the 5- to 600-degree range."

"Right, it was the pan that made the burns," Chief Downs said quickly, his tone going from defensive to offensive. "But what—"

"Hold on a second," Chase said, holding up a finger. "Dr. Trenton, how can you get a cast iron pan that hot? I mean, would a little electric camper stove be sufficient?"

Chief Downs scowled and looked as if he was about to say something, when Martinez calmed him with a stare.

Chase was reminded of her conversation with Floyd, about how he had said that Downs and Martinez went back some time. Floyd might have only met Martinez once before, when he was much younger, but Chase was beginning to think that the two men before her knew each other much better than they were letting on.

"I—I—I don't think so," Dr. Trenton said at last. For the first time since they had arrived in the man's domain, they had taken him out of his comfort zone, and now he wasn't so sure of himself. "I mean, probably not… it might but it would take a long time."

Chase mulled this over. She wasn't much of a cook—that was Brad's territory—but something about what Dr. Trenton said rang true with her. Brad had insisted on a gas stove for this very reason: electric stoves took too long to heat up and they never got hot enough.

"But gas?"

"Gas would be better—more efficient," Dr. Trenton agreed.

Chief Downs crossed his arms over his large stomach. Clearly, he wasn't following along with her train of thought.

"But—*but*," Dr. Trenton continued. His eyes widened, as he caught on. "Even with a small *gas* camping stove, the propane would run out before you got hot enough. You're going to need a lot of energy to get the pan up to six hundred degrees, and then you are going to have to do that four times."

"Four times?" Chief Downs asked.

Dr. Trenton looked at him as if he had four heads.

"For each of their legs. The killer would have to reheat it before he cauterized each of their wounds."

Chief Downs's Adam's apple bobbed as he swallowed hard.

Chapter 15

"WHAT ABOUT THE WOUNDS? Any details on what made them?" Martinez asked.

Dr. Trenton's face morphed back into the epitome of smugness.

"Generic handsaw. Cuts are rough, uneven. I can tell you that Yolanda's left leg was first, followed by her right. Same order for Francine, who was done second—I can tell from the cut marks that it had started to dull considerably by the time the killer got around to her."

Chief Downs swallowed hard again.

"I used to chop down trees in my younger days before I was a cop. Every once in a while, the chainsaw would bind, or I would run out of gas and we would have to resort to using a handsaw. I can tell you, that even cutting a tree as thick as… as… as a leg, it would tire you out something fierce."

Chase nodded; she was thinking the same thing. With this new information, she had a sudden strong desire to see the bodies again. She was hoping that her subconscious—that's what it was, the gut feeling that Agent Jeremy Stitts had been so fond to speak of, it had to be—would put together more pieces to this puzzle.

"So, we're looking for someone in good shape, with at least a rudimentary knowledge of cooking and cooking devices. He drives a Chevy cargo van, which may or may not have some sort of cooking apparatus installed. A converted camping van, perhaps," Martinez said, summing up their new information. Chase got the impression by the far off look in his eyes that he was adding all of this to a refined profile of their killer.

Just don't be too certain… that was our mistake with the Download Killer case, with Colin and Ryanne Elliot.

"I can ask around at some of the local body shops to see if anyone has worked on a Chevy van, fitted one for camping. It's a long shot, but..." Chief Downs let his sentence trail off.

"Sounds good. In the meantime, Agent Adams and—"

The Chief's walkie suddenly squawked, interrupting Martinez. Downs reached for it, and brought it to his mouth.

"Chief Downs," he said, his eyes narrowing.

"Chief? It's Deputy Hascom. I'm out at The Barking Frog."

"Hascom, did you say *Barking Frog*?"

"Yeah, I spoke to Francine's roommates and they said that she was there, with Yolanda, a couple nights ago before she went missing. And guess what? They have cameras."

Even though the Chief had since turned his back to them, the deputy's words came through loud and clear.

"Great—great work. I'm coming down there. Send the address to my phone."

"Uh, Chief? The owner... well, he's kinda being a dick about the whole thing. Says that he won't give up the tapes unless we get a subpoena."

Chase looked at Martinez, who was staring intently at Chief Downs's back.

"Let the prick say what he wants, run his mouth. He might change his tune once I get down there with the feds. Just keep him talking—don't let him go near the tapes."

"Alright. See you soon, Chief. Hascom out."

Chief Downs tucked the walkie back into his belt, then turned to face them.

"That it, Dr. Trenton?"

Dr. Trenton nodded.

"That's all I have for now. Should I forward this information on to...?"

"Send it to me," Martinez said. "I'll have one of my guys in the bureau see if they can find connection between the van, the pan, and the stove."

It sounded like the start of a bad joke to Chase, and she would have laughed.

The van, the pan, and the stove...

Except in this pan, they cooked human flesh. Burned it. Turned it into blackened meat only to keep the victims alive long enough to freeze to death.

Dr. Trenton nodded.

"And I'll have my guys look into the auto shops, see if any of them have fitted a van with a propane stove," Chief Downs added. "You guys coming with me to The Barking Toad?"

Frog... he said The Barking Frog.

"Yep," Martinez replied, rising to his feet.

Chase's brow furrowed.

"You go ahead," she said. "I'm going to go take another look at the bodies."

The corners of Martinez's mouth twitched.

"What for?"

"Just want to see something, is all. Probably nothing. I'll get Floyd to bring me to the bar as soon as I'm done."

"I'll wait for you."

Chase said nothing until Chief Downs snapped his meaty fingers in front of her face.

She startled.

"No, it's okay. I'll catch up. You see if you can help get the owner to give up the tapes."

Martinez looked about to say something, to protest, but Chief Downs stepped between them.

"Fine. Let's go, Chris."

When the two were gone, Chase turned to Dr. Trenton, who had since returned his attention to his computer.

"Dr. Trenton? Can you take me to the morgue to see the bodies? Or are they here now?"

The man didn't turn.

"Hmm?"

Now it was Chase's turn to be frustrated. Dr. Trenton only seemed mildly interested in finding the killer, a monster who had hacked the feet off two college girls, soldered their wounds with a frying pan, and then left them to freeze to death in the snow.

His own life was far more important.

If it doesn't happen to you, it doesn't matter.

Hadn't she heard that once? Wasn't that a saying?

Chase wasn't sure, but thought that if it wasn't, it ought to be.

Why can't you think about us? Brad had asked her long ago, *About Felix, about how he misses his mom? About me? About how I miss you?*

Chase grimaced, and she reached out and laid a hand on Dr. Trenton's shoulder. The man jumped.

"Take me to the bodies," she said sternly.

Chapter 16

"**They're in here,** Dr. Trenton informed her. "Chief Downs asked that they be moved from the morgue to search for more trace evidence once the tire tracks came in."

The man had taken her down the hallway toward a room not unlike the one she had been in yesterday. While back in his domain, safe among his computers and facts, Dr. Trenton had been direct to the point of rude, confident bordering on arrogant, his steps slowed as they walked. By the time they stopped outside the door, his feet barely left the ground. The shuffling sound the man's worn runners made reminded her of Felix when he was younger, when he woke up too early, before the sun was up, and hovered around hers and Brad's bedroom door. Felix knew he would get in trouble if he came right in, or if he spoke, so he just shuffled about until the sound annoyed Chase enough to holler for him to enter.

I should call them again later, she thought, *let them know what's going on, that I won't be home for at least a few days. And Jeremy... I should call Agent Stitts. Ask him how he's doing, see if he can shed some light on the enigma that is Special Agent Chris Martinez.*

Dr. Trenton put his hand on the doorknob and turned it. Only, he didn't open the door; instead, the man simply stood there, waiting for Chase to make the next move.

She frowned.

"You're not coming in?"

Dr. Trenton shook his head.

"No. Can't. Have work to do. Francine and Yolanda are at the back, in the freezer. Their cubbies are clearly marked."

Chase nodded and pushed the door open.

"Once you leave, however, you can't get back in without a card," Dr. Trenton said, holding up his CSU pass for her to see.

Again, Chase nodded. She didn't need to come back in.

One more time would be enough.

One more time was sufficient to find out if what had happened yesterday was a mistake, a fatigue-induced nightmare.

"That's fine. Thank you."

Dr. Trenton grumbled something, but the door was already partway closed, and she couldn't make it out.

With a shrug, Chase turned back to the room.

Yesterday, Yolanda's and Francine's corpses had been on the gurneys out in the open, and Chase was grateful that they were no longer on display like cuts of prime meat.

The room itself reeked of antiseptic cleansers and something else, something that tickled her nostrils and made the back of her throat itch.

What was it that Dr. Beckett Campbell called the preservative they used on bodies nowadays? Not formaldehyde, not anymore, but...

Chase's eyes fell on a white plastic bottle on a table by the side of the room, alongside several medical tools, plastic baggies marked with orange bio-hazard symbols, and specimen containers of the like that Dr. Campbell had used the first time they had met, when he was busy scooping Monarch caterpillars from the mouths of the Butterfly Killer's victims.

Formalin, the bottle read.

Yeah, that was it; not formaldehyde, but formalin.

And it was strong enough to make her head spin.

Chase made it quickly to the back of the room, stopping in front of a row of what looked like locker doors. But these weren't your generic, high school variety, these didn't contain an apple, a textbook, posters of a bare-chested boy bands.

With a swallow, she moved in front of the locker marked, "Strand, Yolanda," grabbed the handle and pulled.

She had expected the smell of funk, of rot and decay, but was pleasantly surprised when this never materialized. In fact, the interior of the locker, or cubby as Dr. Trenton had called it, smelled fresher than the room itself. It was only after she grabbed the handle at chest-height and pulled, and the gurney with Yolanda's body on it slid out, did she realize that a fan was running inside the locker.

And when the body slid all the way out, she heard the fan click off.

Yolanda looked identical to yesterday. Her black skin was still white-washed, as if she had been covered in a fine layer of chalk dust. Her eyes were closed, her hair braided, laying on the steel gurney like the fingers of the dead, splayed, reaching.

Her feet—at least where her feet should have been—were closest to Chase, and she thought she could smell the faint odor of seared flesh.

Despite her expectations, her stomach did a little flip. She told herself that this was in preparation to what might happen again, but she knew in the back of her mind that this wasn't completely true.

It was also the fact that she was in the presence of two dead girls, two beautiful girls attending college, with their entire lives in front of them.

The inside of Chase's left elbow suddenly started to itch, to itch furiously, and if it weren't for the fact that she had put the puffy red jacket that Martinez had given her back on after leaving Dr. Trenton's lair, she might have succumbed to the urge then.

To take her mind off the subject, she reached out and said, "Yolanda."

When her hand came down on Yolanda's calf—her skin was cold, so incredibly cold, like ice covered in a thin layer of plastic—Chase was suddenly transported to another world.

Chapter 17

"I'll do anything... anything at all. And—and I haven't seen your face yet. Neither has Francy. Let us go, we don't even know who you are!"

The man didn't answer. His back was to them, and he was fiddling with something. There was a small hiss, and Yolanda smelled something that reminded her of an old-campfire stove that her uncle had shown her when she was a child.

They used to cook chicken wieners on the small barbecue.

Something told her that she wasn't going to be eating mechanically extruded chicken wrapped in artificial casings this day.

Maybe not ever again.

"Please," she begged. Her eyes flicked over to Francine, but her friend had buried her head in her knees, her bound wrists wrapped around them.

She was rocking slightly, and while it was cold in the back of the van—they were both wearing short skirts when they had been abducted outside the bar—Yolanda knew better than to think that it was only the cold that was affecting her.

There was a click, followed by a small burst of red flame.

What's he doing? What the hell does he want from us?

But in the back of her mind she knew—or at least she thought she knew.

What does any man want from two young women?

The back of the van suddenly started to warm as the heat from the fire spread.

The man reached over and grabbed something form the small shelf, something that glinted in the orange firelight.

"Please, mister. I mean, we'll do anything that you want. Anything. Just promise to let us go."

The man said nothing as he moved the reflective object over the flame.

"I'm... I have a sister and a brother. A mother who loves me," Yolanda continued. She shot looks over at Francine, trying to convince her with her eyes to speak, to humanize themselves in the presence of this monster.

That was their only hope to get out alive. Make him see them as people, as living breathing human beings, people who deserve to remain on this astral plane.

"Mister, I'm only—" twenty-three years old, Yolanda meant to say, but the words got stuck in her throat.

The man whipped around, and she finally realized what the object he had gotten from the shelf was.

A saw.

A metal, triangular wedge of horror that glowed red hot from hovering above the flame.

Yolanda screamed when the man's hand grabbed one of her ankles and pulled her leg straight.

She shrieked loudly when his hands, hands so strong that she would have bet them capable of crushing concrete, squeezed just above her ankle bone.

When she first heard, then a fraction of a second later felt, the sizzle of her skin bubble and boil beneath the hot saw tines, her scream became something inhuman, and all thoughts of humanizing herself in front of this monster scattered in the snow.

***

Chase gasped and pulled her hand off Yolanda's leg.

It happened again; the same visceral feelings and images of yesterday.

It was as if she had *been* Yolanda.

"What the fuck is going on?" she whispered.

Staring down at the body, she reached for the phone in her pocket. She scrolled to Agent Stitts's number and pressed send.

This was his doing; somehow, he had implanted an idea in her mind, something about the subconscious, about evolution and instinct and how these were tools that could be honed to pick up on subtle clues missed by the active mind.

Chase clearly remembered the conversation that had taken place in her BMW.

She also remembered how she had thought it bullshit.

Now, however, it—

"Hello?"

"Jeremy? Thank God you're—"

"—you've reached Jeremy's cell. Please leave a message and I'll get back to you as soon as possible."

"Shit," Chase cursed, just as the phone beeped. "Jeremy, it's Chase. I've got to ask you something—it's about this case, and about what you said in the car a few months back. Something strange is happening—"

Please, we'll do anything if you promise to let us go.

"—give me a call back whenever you have a free second. And thanks; I didn't get a chance to properly thank you for getting me in, and this first case is—"

Chase realized that she was rambling, something that she hadn't done in a long time, and stopped herself before things got out of hand.

"Anyways, give me a call. Please."

Chase hung up, and she turned her eyes back to Yolanda's corpse.

With a swallow, and a strange, silent goodbye, she pushed the tray back in, hearing the fan click on. She latched the locker and then ran her fingers over the name-tag—*Strand, Yolanda - 23 y/o*—before hurrying from the room without looking back.

Outside, she found Floyd leaning up against the front of his Town Car, staring off into the distance. A cigarette dangled between his lips.

He was preoccupied by something and didn't hear or see Chase approach.

"Have one of those for me?" she asked.

Floyd was so startled that he dropped the cigarette. Instead of picking it up, he casually brushed snow on top of it with his boot like a teenager hiding a cigarette from his mother.

"Y-Y-Y-You f-f-frightened me."

"Sorry," Chase said, with a hint of a smile.

"D-d-did you say something?"

Chase resisted the urge to look down at the spot of disturbed snow where Floyd had covered the burning cigarette.

"Just that we should get going."

Floyd nodded, and adjusted his hat.

"Where to?"

"The Barking Frog," she said. "You know it?"

It was Floyd's turn to smirk.

"I'v-v-v-ve heard of it," he said as he made his way to the rear door and held it open for her.

Chapter 18

"**This is it, Ag-g-g-gent Adams,**" Floyd said.

Chase put down her phone, and tucked it into her coat pocket. She tried calling Brad three times, and had called Agent Stitts twice, but neither had answered.

Her eyes drifted from the phone to the window. The snow had stopped falling, and the midmorning was bright with sunshine. Chase was beginning to think that the weather in Anchorage had commitment issues: it was as if the city wanted to be cold, freezing, in fact, but couldn't quite bring itself to fully commit to it.

Twisted tubes of glass filled with whatever gas gave the words *The Barking Frog* their bright green glow, didn't help the illusion either. It felt like a bar that should be located in Hawaii or the Virgin Gorda or some other tropical location that Chase had never been, and not in the heart of Anchorage. But, Chase supposed as she thanked Floyd for the ride, that this was likely the proprietor's intentions.

The intention, as it turned out, was to get college girls inside the bar.

Get them inside and then get them drunk.

That much Chase ascertained from just stepping through the large, chrome doors and into an interior that she suspected might have moonlighted as a warehouse had moonlighting not been its primary form of business.

Job number one: get girls inside.

Job number two: get them drunk.

Just inside the front doors was a giant tub filled with ice, and off to one side, lit in equally as phosphorescent bulbs as the outdoor signage, was a bar. It wasn't even quite ten in the morning and yet the place seemed busy. She suspected that it wouldn't open until later, but there was much to be done, it seemed. The bar was presently being stocked by a man in a white T-shirt—young, with a thick beard that was neatly combed—while another, much larger and older man was fussing with the lines leading to the beer taps. Chase inspected the two men for a moment, listening closely to the sound of bottles clinking together, the hiss of CO_2 from a hidden tube.

    She imagined the place packed, Yolanda and Francine dancing, sweating maybe, their skin covered in a sheen of sweat and alcohol.

    "Not open until three," the man behind the bar, the young, good-looking one, informed her.

    Chase looked up and smiled.

    The man smiled back.

    "Come back then and I'll give you a couple free drinks. Bring your friends and I'll give you all shots," he said without losing his grin. He had the most stunning green eyes that seemed soft and caring.

    Chase didn't want to smile anymore but couldn't seem to help herself. She had been in the presence of charming men before and knew that charm was nothing but a skill that people used to influence the way others behaved around them—Agent Stitts had said as much—but this knowledge did nothing to limit her susceptibility to it. And this man, this bartender, oozed charm like a turtle oozed tranquility.

    "I'm not sure you'd want my friends coming here tonight," Chase said.

    The man shrugged.

    "If they're anything like you, as pretty as you are, then I'm sorry, but they're *exactly* the clientele that we want."

    The man turned the label on a Tito's vodka bottle so that it pointed out toward the bar, and then hopped down. He wiped his hands on a white towel that hung from his hip and started toward her.

"Too often this place is filled with college girls that…" he raised an eyebrow, "how can I say this politely? Let's just say that at night the girls and the booze flow loosely."

Chase said nothing as he approached. He moved slowly, without haste, but with purpose in a nonaggressive manner.

Oh, he's good.

From just this small sample size, Chase could tell that he was smart, too smart maybe, to be a bartender. But she also got the impression that the *loose*—his word—women that he had just admonished were one of the main reasons he worked here.

"I'll tell you what," he said, lowering his voice and glancing around furtively, "I'm not supposed to do this, but if you want a drink now, I can probably hook you up."

Chase opened her mouth, but he held up a manicured finger and halted her speech before it began.

"But you have to promise to come back later, okay?"

The man started to backpedal toward the bar.

"That's awfully kind of you, but I'm afraid I can't."

The bartender stopped.

"Can't what? Can't come back or can't get your friends to come back? Tonight's going—"

"Can't have a drink. I'm on the job."

Another eyebrow raise, only this one was in genuine surprise and not part of his act.

Chase pulled her badge out of her pocket and flipped it open. The man's green eyes darted from the FBI emblem, to Chase's face, and back to the badge.

His mouth fell open.

"I'm so sorry, I—" he cleared his throat and suddenly grew serious. "Your friends are in the back with Tony."

Chase smirked.

"That's alright, I'm sure they have it under control. What's your name, by the way?"

Suddenly guarded, the man seemed to shrink into himself. "Brent."

Chase extended a hand and the man took a step forward and shook it. His grip was weak, his hand moist. Clearly, he wasn't used to not being the one in charge.

"Chase Adams, FBI. Can you direct me to the bathroom, please?"

The man looked confused, but then pointed down a long, dark hallway beside the bar.

"It's down there. But there's a staff bathroom that might be—"

Chase waved a hand.

"I'm sure this one's fine," Chase said. "Thanks, Brent."

With that, she turned and headed down the hallway.

As she walked, Chase tried to imagine the music blaring, Yolanda and Francine, holding hands maybe, making their way through a crowd of sweaty wall-huggers as they made their way to the restroom. No vision came, at least nothing like what had happened back with the bodies, but she thought she did a fairly good job of recreating the scene from her own college days.

There was a sign on the wall up ahead, the typical silhouette of a woman in a dress indicating that the female bathroom was this way, and she followed it down the hallway.

Outside the door, however, Chase paused.

There was a collage of photographs on the wall, tucked within a glass case that looked thick enough to stop a bullet. She stopped in front of it, her eyes scanning the images.

All three or four dozen photos were of women, most with red eyes, tongues out, colored drinks gripped in manicured fingers. Some of them were kissing, women playing up the scene as they were no doubt encouraged to do by Brent the Bartender.

Chase pressed a hand on the bathroom door and was about to push it open, when a picture in the bottom right hand corner of the case caught her eye.

"What the hell?"

She leaned in close, and then recoiled.

The woman in the picture was smiling, her perfect white teeth standing out against her dark skin.

Chase's jaw fell open.

It was Yolanda Strand.

Chapter 19

CHASE HURRIED BACK TO the bar, and called out to Brent, who had since returned to organizing bottles of liquor.

"Hey," she said, her throat suddenly dry. She hooked a thumb over her shoulder when he turned to face her. "Those pictures—"

"The ones by the bathroom? Yeah, they're pretty dumb, I know. I've asked to take them down, but the owner nixed that idea. The customers—the girls—they like them. It's like Instagram in the real world, you know?"

Chase shook her head, trying to focus.

"But who puts them in there? Do you take the pictures here, or do—"

Brent jumped off the bar again.

"I put them in there, why?" he asked, concern etched on his face.

Chase swallowed hard again, feeling dizzy. She regretted turning down the drink offer, on the job or not.

"The girl—the one in the corner—the one with the—" she made a gesture toward her hair, trying to make a braid, but realized that this was probably not making any sense to the man. "Come with me," she settled on, heading back toward the bathroom.

Chase stopped outside the case of photos, and jabbed a finger at Yolanda.

"This girl… did you take this picture?"

Brent shrugged.

"I told you, I took all the pictures. Maybe one or two of them the other—"

"Do you know her?"

Brent reached for her hand, but she pulled away sharply before his fingers touched her skin.

"Sorry," he said softly, "just couldn't see—your finger was on it. Yeah, I know her. That's Yolanda."

Chase turned to face him. His handsome features were pinched slightly, the inner corners of his eyebrows moving a fraction of an inch up his forehead.

"You *know* her?"

Brent nodded hesitantly.

"Yeah, Yolanda. She comes in here every Thursday. Usually with her friend... uh, uh, Francy, or something like that. Why? What's this about? Does it have to do with why the FBI are—"

Chase reached for his arm and grabbed his bicep. His muscles were thick and strong, and while she intended to pull him roughly, the man barely noticed.

"I think we need to talk," Chase said as she started toward the bar.

"Yeah, sure," Brent replied, shrugging her off. "What's this about? Is Yolanda okay?"

Chase said nothing until she was again highlighted by the fluorescent lights behind the bar.

"Where are the other Agents?" she asked, ignoring the question.

"In the back with Tony."

"Where?" Chase snapped.

"In the back," Brent repeated. He raised a hand and pointed around the other side of the bar. At the end of the hallway was what looked like a reinforced door. "They're in the security room."

"Take me there," Chase demanded.

Brent did as he was instructed.

When they reached the door, she knocked twice.

"Agent Adams," she said loudly.

The door opened, and Martinez peered out. He looked at her, then at Brent.

"Who's this?"

"The bartender—he *knew* Yolanda."

Martinez's eyes narrowed, and he opened his mouth to say something, when Brent suddenly reacted violently, pulling away from the door.

"Knew? What do you mean *knew*?" His eyes were wide, and any remnants of the charisma he had shown when Chase had first walked into The Barking Frog were gone.

Martinez, noticing this visceral reaction, stepped out of the room.

"I think we need to chat," he said.

Brent was breathing heavily now.

"What happened to Yolanda?"

Chase watched Brent closely as Martinez approached him.

"We just want to talk," Martinez said, his hands out at his sides.

Brent looked scared—scared and alarmed.

Chase was reminded of the preliminary profile that Agent Martinez had provided Chief Downs and his crew.

A charming man, someone that the girls would have trusted.

Was this their guy?

He had charm, that was certain. And who didn't trust a bartender? People routinely opened up to them, telling complete strangers the impetus behind them sidling up at the bar on a Wednesday before noon.

"Please, just tell me what happened to her. Is she injured? Is she—"

Agent Martinez suddenly broke into a run. He bumped into Chase as he passed, pushing her up against the wall. The breath was forced from her lungs, and a pain shot up her hip.

Brent, eyes still wide, instinctively turned and started to bolt, but Martinez was on him before he had taken more than a handful of steps.

His shoulder slammed into Brent's back, and both men went sprawling to the ground. The commotion drew Chief Downs from the security room, and he moved his considerable girth past Chase, who was still struggling to catch her breath, and toward the two downed men.

Martinez grabbed Brent's left arm and twisted it behind his back. Brent was strong, and he struggled mightily, but Martinez lowered his weight between the man's shoulder blades, pressing down on him.

"Stop moving!" he shouted. "*Stop moving!*"

Chase watched this with earnest, her heart racing in her chest. Behind her, she heard someone approaching, someone who was also breathing heavily.

Instincts took over, and she slid the pistol from her holster and spun around.

The man who moved toward her looked like an overweight accountant, with a gray mustache and thinning hair. He was a large man, not as large as Chief Downs, but it was clear that he didn't miss too many meals.

"Don't move," Chase said, vaguely aware that her hand was trembling. The accountant's arms rocketed upward.

"Easy! Easy! I'm not doing anything wrong here!"

And yet he continued to stride forward.

"Stop!" Chase shouted.

The man didn't listen. His body language was one of complacency, but he continued to approach nonetheless.

Chase's finger moved to the trigger.

"You take one more—"

A hand gently came down on the top of the pistol.

"It's okay, Agent Adams," Chief Downs said.

Hearing his voice, Chase lowered the gun and turned to face him.

Her breathing was coming in short bursts, and the entire ordeal since seeing Yolanda's photograph, suddenly felt strange to her.

What the hell am I doing?

Her hand shook so badly now that it was a blur, and it took four tries to put the pistol securely back in her holster.

"Jesus, take it easy, lady," the large man, who Chase now pegged was the manager or owner, said.

Chief Downs came between them, and Martinez spoke up next.

"I'm going to take Brent in for questioning," he said.

Chase saw that Brent had been put in cuffs, and his head was lowered.

"This is crazy," the owner/manager said. "He didn't do anything."

Martinez shook his head.

"I'm taking him in for questioning, that's all. And then I'll be back… back with a warrant for those tapes. You better hope I don't find anything on them or I will take you in too." He lifted Brent's arms from behind, and the man winced. "And you think this is bad? Just wait to see what happens to you next."

Chapter 20

CHASE WAS STILL SHAKING when she finally made it back to Floyd's car.

"Y-Y-You okay?"

She was getting annoyed with that question, and took a deep breath.

He means well, she told herself. *But the other two? Chief Downs and Agent Martinez? With those two, she wasn't so sure.* They both seemed to have their own agendas, ones that clearly didn't include keeping her involved.

What's the point of me being here if I can't even do my job? If they won't let me in?

"Fine," she snapped back.

Floyd's eyes drifted to the mirror, but he caught wind of her attitude and resisted saying anything else other than, "Where to?"

Chase bit her tongue.

Home, she almost said. *Take me home to my husband and son.*

"The precinct. Take me to the precinct."

Images of Yolanda flashed in her mind, and she shook her head, trying to clear her thoughts as Floyd pulled away from The Barking Frog.

Why is this affecting me so much? she wondered.

She hadn't even felt this way when Dr. Mark Kruk, the infamous Butterfly Killer, had taken her hostage, intending on making her his final victim.

She had been scared then, terrified even, but this… this was different somehow. It was as if she had been Yolanda, really *been* her, and that she had died.

Her feet had been hacked off, the wounds cauterized, and then Chase had been left to freeze to death in the snow.

I'm dead.

The thought carried so much impact that Chase felt a tear spill down her cheek. She turned her face to the window, and then swiped the tear away with the back of her hand.

What's wrong with me?

With a shaking hand, she pulled her cell phone out of her pocket.

Please have a missed call, a text at least.

But as she stared at the screen, her heart sunk further. There were no missed calls, no texts, no messages whatsoever. Loneliness was like an ill-fitting glove, one that only served to annoy rather than to offer comfort and warmth.

Her thumb hovered over the button, before Chase eventually pressed it and unlocked the phone.

All she wanted was someone to talk to, someone to share what she was feeling with.

Her first instinct was to call Agent Stitts, then her husband. But for some reason, she hesitated on both fronts.

Never in her life had she felt so alone.

Instead, she scrolled down to a person she thought might be able to help her.

With a deep, hitching breath, she clicked the name and waited. After two rings, a man answered.

"Drake? It's Chase. I need... I need someone to talk to. You have a minute?"

"It's nice to hear your voice," Damien Drake replied. "What's up?"

***

Invigorated, Chase stepped out of the Town Car and made her way toward the precinct with determined steps. Her conversation with Drake had soothed her mind, at least temporarily.

It had also given her perspective.

There was a killer on the loose, and that killer might just be Brent the Bartender.

The rest could wait.

Agent Martinez had told her that they intended to interview Brent in Room 3, which is where she headed to directly.

As she neared the room, however, two of Chief Downs's men stood blocking the door.

"Agent Adams," the first said. Chase nodded, and then reached for the door.

The man didn't move—he remained blocking her path.

"Chief Downs wants you to watch from the observation room," he said, indicating another door next to the one he stood in front of.

Chase frowned. She wanted to be in there with Brent, to see his face, gauge his reactions, not observe from behind a thick pane of glass.

Her eyes narrowed.

"I want to speak to him."

The man misunderstood what she meant, and said, "Chief Downs says it's best for you to just watch this one. Too many people in the—"

She shook her head.

"No. I want to speak to Downs."

The officer's face twisted, and Chase got the impression that Downs wouldn't react kindly to the interruption.

But she had the badge, didn't she? A nice badge with her name on it, followed by the letters *F*, *B*, and *I*.

"He said—"

Chase squinted at the man. He was young, younger than her even, and was just trying to do his job.

"Tell him I need to speak to him," she repeated. The officer swallowed, then reluctantly turned to the door.

"Please," he said, looking back at her, "Wait in the observation room, at least."

Chase considered this for a moment before agreeing. Burning bridges to get what she wanted was one thing but setting the entire town alight wouldn't serve her any good. As the officer entered the interrogation room, Chase pulled the adjacent door wide and stepped inside, observing the scene from behind glass.

Brent, no longer cuffed, sat in a chair that looked as if it was made of welded coat hangers. A sheen of sweat covered his face and forehead, and his posture was slumped, dejected.

Agent Martinez stood off to one side, propping himself up against the wall with his foot. The officer that Chase had just spoken with was presently conversing with Chief Downs. Downs was leaning over him, his shadow completely engulfing the other man.

The officer looked more frightened than Brent did.

After saying his piece, Chief Downs barked something that was inaudible then looked over to Martinez.

Agent Martinez chewed his lip for a moment then shook his head.

Downs smirked, then waved the other officer away.

"What the fuck?" Chase mumbled. She reached over and pressed the button marked *Room 3 Audio*.

The officer left the room and closed the door, and then, instead of following him out as Chase had expected, Downs planted two meaty hands on the table and pressed down on it.

His considerable gut sagged and rested on the table between his palms.

"Brent Pine… Brent Pine…" the Chief said almost thoughtfully. "Let me ask you something… you have a foot fetish, Brent?"

Chase cringed at the associated imagery, but her eyes remained locked on Brent's handsome face.

The man's lips twisted in confusion.

"Foot fetish? Wha—what are you talking about?"

Chief Downs frowned.

"You know exactly what I'm talking about. *Foot fetish*. I bet you get to enact all sorts of weird fantasies working at that bar, don't you?"

Brent was no longer the charming man tending The Barking Frog, Chase realized. That had just been a front. Now, he was just scared.

"I don't know what you're talking about. Is Yolanda okay? Did something happen to her?"

Downs laughed and looked over at Martinez again, who was also studying Brent intently.

"You hear that, Chris? Brent Pine, *handsome* Brent Pine, is acting innocent, isn't he? Acting like he doesn't know what happened to those girls."

Brent leaned even further away from the Police Chief.

"I don't… I really don't—"

"Oh, you don't, do you? Maybe we can jog your memory, then."

Chief Downs stood up straight—Chase actually thought she saw the table rebound just a little as his weight lifted—and went to Agent Martinez, who produced a file folder from somewhere behind him.

As the Chief strode back toward Brent, there was a knock on the observation room door.

"Yeah?" Chase said over her shoulder. The door opened, and the officer with whom she had spoken with moments ago appeared, looking pale.

"Chief Downs said… well, he said he would speak to you *after*."

Chase didn't turn around.

Instead, she continued to focus on Brent and the Police Chief.

The latter opened the folder and then shoved it over to Brent. From her vantage point, Chase couldn't see exactly what the images were, but she knew that they must have been of Yolanda and Francine.

"What is—" Brent suddenly went completely white. "I'm going to be sick," he gasped.

Chief Downs pouted dramatically.

"Oh, now you're going to be sick, but at the time—"

"Agent Adams?" the officer behind her said. "Did you hear what I said?"

Frustrated by the interruption, Chase spun around.

"What? What do you—"

The officer's walkie chirped, cutting her off mid-sentence.

"Officer Greenwald?"

The young man tore the walkie from his belt.

"Yeah?"

"We found the van… we found the van outside Brent Pine's house."

Chase gasped.

Chapter 21

A‍GENT M‍ARTINEZ OFFERED TO drive Chase to the van outside Brent Pine's house, which left Floyd standing empty-handed outside the precinct. For some reason, Chase felt bad for him; it was clear that for once in his life, Floyd was finally finding himself useful, that he was needed by someone.

Any reservations or suspicions that Chase might have harbored for him had long since vanished; he was a simple man, one that, like her, needed to feel important, like he had a role to play in the world around him.

That he could affect things, and wasn't just simply along for the ride.

Chase momentarily debated declining Martinez's offer and going with Floyd instead, but decided that that would be unwise: their relationship, if it could be called as such, was already strained, and if their partnership was to work there would be some give and take involved.

Chase, however, thought that she was likely the one to do most of the giving, at least for the time being.

She apologized to Floyd and went with Martinez.

Guided by a train of police cars, Martinez pulled out of the precinct parking lot, and followed.

Three times Chase opened her mouth to say something but couldn't find the right words. In the end, it was Martinez who spoke up first.

"He fits the profile," he said simply. "Young, good-looking. No record. Probably convinced the girls to stay after the bar closed. Maybe slipped something into their drinks."

"But the tox came back relatively clean," Chase replied instinctively.

Martinez shrugged.

"No idea how long they were held captive for. Might have cleared their system by the time they died."

Chase chewed the inside of her lip. Martinez was right and, besides, she had witnessed the man's charm and charisma firsthand.

Brent Pine *definitely* fit the profile.

So why did she feel in the pit of her stomach that he wasn't their guy?

"I can see it in your face," Martinez continued as he pulled onto the highway. "You don't think he did it."

Again, Chase started to say something, but bit her tongue. She wasn't sure if it was the way that Chief Downs had brushed her off, or how Martinez had shaken his head when she had demanded to speak to them in the observation room, but something felt wrong here.

It was too easy.

Could Brent Pine be a mastermind manipulator, a sadistic torturer, and yet be foolish enough to abduct the girls from the bar, *his* bar, a bar with cameras no less, and then leave the murder van outside his home?

No, it was way too easy.

Something occurred to her then.

"Hey, did you manage to subpoena the tapes from the night the girls went missing?"

Martinez shook his head.

"Not yet—left that to Downs and his men. But now with the van, it should be a slam dunk."

Chase nodded and turned to the window. The train of cop cars lit up the sky, and the dark clouds that threatened above reflected their combined purple color. It was only midafternoon, but dark came early in Anchorage, and the foreboding weather wasn't helping any.

"I know what you're thinking… that he couldn't be this stupid."

Chase looked back at Martinez, whose eyes were locked on the road, surprise on her face. Martinez, evidently, knew *exactly* what she was thinking.

"Something like that," Chase conceded. She still felt the need to be guarded around her partner.

"I've been at this game for a long time, Chase."

So you keep telling me…

And while she had no reason not to believe Martinez, it dawned on her that she knew nothing about him. *Absolutely* nothing. How long had he been with the FBI, for instance? How old was he?

Floyd had mentioned something about him having a sister who used to live here, but what about other family? Was he married? Did he have children?

Chase wasn't the poster-child for openness, certainly, but he seemed to know about her.

"And one of the things that I learned early on," he continued, "is that there isn't always a demented, yet somehow noble, motive for these murders. You need to come to terms with the fact that there are just bad people out there who are destined to do bad things."

Martinez paused, and his head tilted to one side just a little.

"And sometimes people do bad things just because they can."

Chase mulled this over. She wasn't as naive as Martinez made her out to be and was reminded of her time as a Narc in Seattle.

The man's name had been Tyler Tisdale, and he grew up in an upscale neighborhood close to the Vancouver border, and was raised by two professional parents. By all accounts, Tyler and his two sisters, both younger than he, had a decent if stale upbringing. Background checks revealed no evidence, not even a hint of molestation or abuse. And yet, at some point, things went wrong for Tyler. It started with taking drugs, but when his parents figured out what he was doing with his allowance, they turned off the faucet, so to speak. As cash grew tight, it became easier for him to start dealing and cutting what he dealt to feed his own habit, as was often the case. Somewhere along the way, Tyler's descent into darkness degenerated to pimping, and his crack den slowly transitioned into a whorehouse.

It was Tyler who Chase tried to expose when she'd gone undercover. It was Tyler who had given her her first hit of heroin, and it was also Tyler with whom she had first traded her body as a commodity.

During this time, Chase had met Tyler's youngest sister, Amy Tilsdale.

Tyler was pimping her out to the highest bidder and had her hooked on meth to keep her under his control.

Just fourteen years young. Jesus; fourteen.

Yeah, Chase knew that sometimes ordinary people did bad things just because. And yet despite this, something in her gut suggested that Brent Pine just wasn't their guy.

Instead of beleaguering this point, Chase decided to change the subject.

"You said that you spoke to Agent Stitts recently? Because I've been trying to reach him..."

Martinez turned back to the road, and Chase followed his stare. The sky was alight with police cherries, and they slowed for a roadblock.

"Yeah, he's the one who put in a good word for you."

"But have you heard from him recently? Because I can't get a hold of him."

Martinez shrugged and rolled down the window.

A police officer shone his flashlight inside the vehicle and Martinez shielded his eyes with the blade of his hand. Then he pulled out his FBI badge and showed it to the officer.

"Agent Martinez," the man said, lowering his flashlight. "Chief Downs said you'd be arriving." He flicked the light quickly in Chase's direction. "Who's this?"

"FBI Special Agent Adams," Martinez replied. "The van here?"

The officer nodded.

"Just up the road, parked on the street. Waiting for you guys to arrive as per the Chief's instructions."

"CSU here?"

"Yeah, waiting."

"Alright, let us through then," Martinez said, and the officer stepped away from the car.

Chase stared out the window at the police officers, most of them leaning up against their vehicles, hands crossed over their jacket-covered chests, bored expressions on their lined faces.

They were all waiting for them… they were waiting for the FBI to swoop in, confirm that this was the same van that was used to kidnap and torture the girls, and to put the final nail in Brent Pine's coffin.

Please… we'll do anything. If you let us go, we'll do anything…

A shudder ran through her as the van loomed into view. Illuminated with large, bright lights that CSU had erected, it looked like some sort of prehistoric relic instead of just a shitty white van, cursed by the elements.

"That's it," she whispered.

Martinez nodded and slammed the car into park.

"That's it," he confirmed. "That's Brent Pine's van, the last place that Yolanda and Francine saw."

Chapter 22

"Open it," Agent Martinez instructed.

The man in the thick gloves and navy coat emblazoned with "Crime Scene Unit" on the back nodded and stepped forward. He grabbed the door handle and pulled it wide.

Chase inhaled sharply.

The interior of the van was almost exactly as she had seen it in her visions.

The metal floor was covered in brown stains—*Yolanda's blood… Yolanda's and Francine's*—and there was a rudimentary stove affixed to one side.

Martinez flicked on his flashlight and strode forward, fully illuminating the interior.

"Van is registered to Brent Pine," an officer behind them stated. "And the neighbors confirm that they've seen him driving it. Says that he lends it out quite a bit to friends who want to go camping, but not recently."

Martinez grunted. His flashlight revealed a heavy cast iron pan tucked behind a large stove.

"This is his van, all right."

"Neighbors say it's been parked here since Tuesday."

Chase's thoughts turned to the no parking signs she had seen as Martinez had pulled onto the street.

"Any tickets?" she asked quietly as she continued to search the van with her eyes.

"Two; for parking violations. Was scheduled to be booted with a third."

Martinez shone the light on the stove, and then followed a series of a metal tubes that ascended upward before leaving out the side of the van.

"Where's the propane?" he asked.

"Dunno. There's a spot for them on the side, but they aren't there. Neighbors heard some noise the other night—likely someone came and took them."

Chase shook her head and blinked rapidly.

This doesn't make any sense. Brent kidnaps the girls, drives out to the deserted road and maims them, dumps their bodies in the snow. Then he comes back here, parks the van illegally, and goes back to work only to return later. He sees the tickets and, instead of moving the van, he just removes the propane?

No, something definitely wasn't adding up. Brent might be a demented psychopath, but from even their brief encounter, Chase knew that he wasn't this stupid.

No one was this stupid.

"Alright, let's get—" Martinez began, but then stopped. He pulled off one of his gloves and reached into his pocket and removed his cell phone.

He brought it to his ear and Chase observed him say a few words, nothing of substance, before hanging up.

Then Martinez turned to her, a scowl on his face.

"I have to go," he said bluntly.

Chase gawked.

"What? What do you mean, you have to go?"

"I have to go," Martinez repeated. Then to the others, he said. "CSU, I want the van to be analyzed with a fine-toothed comb. Go over everything, I want DNA, anything that you can find. Nothing gets through here. We need Brent and Yolanda and Francine to be placed in the van at the same time. Got it?"

There was a series of affirmative grunts, and then Martinez started back toward his car.

It took Chase a few seconds to break out of her stupor.

"Wait up!" she hollered as she hurried after him. She caught him as he was opening the door.

"What… what should I do?"

Martinez chewed his lip.

"Process the van, then interview Brent again. Chief Downs will take care of the rest."

He lowered himself into his seat as Chase watched on, confused.

Martinez closed the door and had already put the car into drive before Chase finally brought herself to ask the question that was on the tip of her tongue.

"Where the hell are you going?"

But Martinez was already gone.

Chapter 23

"I'm trying to understand this, Brent. I really am. But… it's your van and their blood is in it. All over it. And unless you can explain that, then…" Chase let her sentence trail off.

Brent Pine took a deep breath, and then rubbed his eyes. He was exhausted, both mentally and physically.

"I—I don't—" Brent's lawyer gently grabbed his arm.

"You don't have to answer any more questions," he said. Brent shook his arm free.

"But I *want* to. I mean, this is ridiculous. I didn't do any of this… Yolanda and Francine, they were my *friends*."

Chase heard Chief Downs breathing on the back of her neck become more rapid.

"This how you treat—"

Chase shook her head. It was bad enough that he was in the room, but with these regular outbursts, they were going to lose Brent. He would just collapse into a shell and then only his lawyer would be doing the speaking, which would get them nowhere.

But it had been like pulling teeth for Chase to even convince the big Police Chief to let her interview the man, despite Martinez passing the case on to her.

"Okay, fine, let's talk about something else, then? How did you know Yolanda and Francine?"

Brent looked at her with rheumy eyes. He licked his lips, and she grabbed a glass of water and offered it to him.

"Here, drink this."

She heard Chief Downs grunt and knew what he was thinking: *let the bastard dehydrate… let him suffer the way he made those girls suffer.*

Brent drank hungrily, the liquid splashing down his bearded chin.

When he was done, he wiped his mouth with the back of his wrists, which were now chained together.

"Tell me how you knew the girls."

Brent spoke slowly and clearly.

"I met them about a year ago. They came into the bar and I struck up a conversation with Yolanda, and some of her friends."

"That's it?"

Brent shrugged.

"Well, we had a few drinks and then I gave—"

He stopped mid-sentence and then glanced nervously at his lawyer.

"What? You gave them what, Brent?"

The lawyer, a hairless creature with thick black spectacles, held up a finger as he leaned close to his client's ear and whispered something.

Brent nodded, then whispered something back. The lawyer interlaced his fingers.

"My client is exercising his right for silence at this point."

Chase's eyes narrowed.

"Why now? What did you give them, Brent?"

"Again," the lawyer repeated in a monotonous drone, "my client is exc—"

Chief Downs suddenly slammed his hands on the table.

"What did you give them, you little shit? You give them their feet back, huh? No, you didn't give them back, because we never found them. You twisted bastard. You give them a nice grope before you killed them? We know you couldn't get it up enough to—"

"This is borderline harassment, and if you continue—"

"Shut up! Tell us what—"

Brent's face suddenly went red.

"I gave them a fucking bump, that's all. Goddamn it, I didn't do *this!*"

Chase felt her body tense.

He gave them some coke, that's why they became friends. That, and his charm… his charisma.

The lawyer reached out and tried to quiet his client, but Brent had been pushed too far.

"That's it! *One bump!*"

Chief Downs piped in.

"Oh, I bet—"

"Brent, I don't care about a little bit of coke. Really, I don't. I'm FBI, and I'm investigating a double-homicide. And Chief Downs," she turned and looked up at the man, surprised that his fat face had turned deep red, "well, he doesn't care either. So you gave them a bump? So what? They're college girls, if they don't get it from you, they'll just get it from some other shady character."

The words triggered something in Chase's mind then, and she was suddenly transported back to a different time.

The room was dark and dank, reeking of sweat and sour alcohol. Her clothes stank, as did her hair, both of which retained the caustic smell of smoke.

She wasn't alone, Chase knew this, and yet it was difficult for her to make out anything in the dimly lit room.

"Chase? You want a hit of this?"

A meaty palm came down on Chase's shoulder and she jumped.

"I, uh, was that the only time that you gave the girls drugs?" she asked quickly, hoping that the others, unlike Chief Downs who had deliberately touched her shoulder, hadn't noticed her mind drifting.

Brent's lip curled, but he eventually answered.

"No, maybe... maybe once or twice more, but that's it, I swear. Their friend..." he shook his head. "No, that's it."

Chase stared intently as the man spoke. His eyes drifted up and to the right, just a little, indicating that he was recalling rather than fabricating a memory.

"Alright, fine. We got that. But the van... why was their blood in the van?"

Again, ignoring the urgings of his lawyer, Brent answered the question.

"I don't know. I really don't. I lent the van out... didn't even know it was back yet."

"Who'd you lend it to?" Chief Downs hissed over her shoulder.

Before Brent answered, Chase felt the phone in her pocket buzz. She reached in and rejected the call without looking at who it was.

"I don't... I don't know," Brent said, sounding dejected.

"You don't know?" there was a hint of sardonic humor in the Chief's tone now. "Let me get this straight: you lent your van to someone, but you don't know who?"

Brent's body sagged.

"It was a friend of a friend... I don't mind lending it out, it's great for camping and—"

"Camping in the winter, Brent?" Chase asked.

Her phone buzzed again, and she frowned, ignoring it once more.

Brent tried to throw his arms up, but he had forgotten that they were handcuffed, and he winced as the metal bit into his wrists.

"I don't know! I didn't ask!"

Chase hesitated, eyes still fixed on the young man across from her. When he had said he didn't know, that he didn't ask, he had glanced at his lawyer again.

It was the same look he had given when he had first hesitated before telling them about the coke he had sold to Yolanda and Francine.

And then it clicked.

Chase stood, and looked over at the Chief, tilting her head toward the door to indicate that they should take a break.

"I need to use the rest room," she told Brent and his lawyer. "Do you want anything? Coffee? Snack?"

Brent shook his head softly.

"Just some more water, please."

"Sure."

With that, she left the room, thankful that Chief Downs followed her out. When the door closed behind them, she turned to face him.

"He lent the van out, either because it was being used to ship drugs, or he was trading its services for drugs," she whispered. "Either way, drugs are the reason why his van went missing."

The Chief's thick eyebrows furrowed.

"You're not buying this shit, are you? The little fucking twerp—"

"I didn't say that Brent didn't kill them," she said curtly. "Only that the reason why the van was gone was because it was being used to move product."

"And how could you know that?"

Chase opened her mouth and then closed it again.

She knew because she had seen it in the man's face, but she couldn't say that. Especially given the way Downs had looked at her when she had touched Yolanda's leg and then asked them to search for tire tracks belonging to Brent Pine's van.

Agent Stitts might believe in intuition and gut feelings, but the only gut feeling that Chief Downs got was indigestion.

"I used to be a Narc," she said, "I know how dealers behave."

This wasn't entirely true, at least not in this context. She *had* been a Narc, but her true insight into the workings of dealers and addicts had come from—

Her phone buzzed and this time she took it out of her pocket, thinking—*hoping*—that it might be Brad finally returning her call.

"One sec," she said, turning her back to the red-faced police chief.

It wasn't Brad; the number was unlisted.

She answered it.

"Hello?"

"Agent Adams, it's Martinez. I need you here."

Chase plugged her other ear to block out the Chief's mouth-breathing, and hunched over.

"What? Where? What's going on?"

"Can't tell you over the phone. Floyd will pick you up, take you straight to the airport."

Airport?

Chase's head was spinning. She was just starting to get somewhere with the case, and now *this*.

How can the FBI work this way? Swoop in, lay some groundwork and then just leave the inept local PD in charge?

"Leave the case to Chief Downs. He and his men can handle it. It's a slam dunk."

Chase's eyes flicked to Downs, and doubt didn't so much as creep over her as it blanketed her soul.

"I'm not sure that—"

"Finish up there, Floyd will arrive in twenty."

And with that, the line went dead, leaving Chase to stare at the blank screen.

What the hell is going on? What the hell have I gotten myself into?

Chapter 24

"W-w-we need to h-hur-hurry," Floyd said, as he waited for Chase to enter through the door he held open. "You're f-f-flight is in an hou-hou-hour."

Chase nodded and tucked the front of her red jacket closed before stepping inside.

All she had with her was her purse, filled with a couple of extra things—toothbrush, hairbrush, perfume—that she had picked up from the local pharmacy and the gun box that Martinez had given her.

She tossed both onto the seat and buckled up as Floyd shut the door and hurried around to the driver seat.

Chase stared at the shitty hotel through the falling snow. It was not a place she was going to miss.

Neither was the cold.

"Delta f-f-f-light 0231 to Logan Ai-ai-ai-ai-," he knocked the side of his head with the palm of his hand, "Airport."

"Thanks, Floyd."

For once, Floyd was relatively quiet as they drove, and it dawned on her that he was probably going to miss her.

And as a strange as it sounded, Chase thought she was going to miss him too.

But what was she to do? Take him with her? She didn't even know what the hell was going on half the time, how was she supposed to bring someone along for the ride?

And could she even do that? Have her own personal chauffeur? She thought not but, the truth was, Chase had no idea how things at the FBI actually worked.

It's just a test… like with Agent Stitts. Martinez is testing you, and if you pass all shall be revealed.

Chase shook her head and turned her thoughts to the strangeness of the case that she was abandoning. Brent Pine had allegedly murdered those two girls, and Agent Martinez had promptly skipped town, leaving it up to an ill-tempered and reactionary Police Chief to wrap things up.

At least in New York, she got to see things through. It often took a long time to get there, but Chase would eventually testify on the stand. In fact, this had been the case in both New York and Seattle.

But this... this just nab the bad guy and get up and leave? This was new.

And she hated it.

Agent Martinez, on the other hand, didn't seem at all bothered by it.

I've been doing this a long time, Chase. A long, long time.

Chase recalled the expression on his face as they stood behind Brent's kill van, the way he had frowned as he answered his phone, the call that had drawn him away, evidently to Boston.

Had it been a frown? Yes, she was fairly certain that it was. But there was something else in that expression, something in the way his lips twisted at the corners.

But what?

Satisfaction?

Relief?

"Hey Floyd?"

"Yes, m-m-ma'am?"

"You told me before that Chief Downs and Martinez go way back?"

"Yes, ma'am. Like I said, M-M-Martinez used to live here a c-c-couple of years ago."

Chase chewed her lip.

"But he's not original to Alaska, is he?"

She wasn't certain, but Chase thought she detected a hint of a Midwestern accent in her partner's voice.

"No, he moved here with his sister."

This took Chase by surprise, and she blinked.

"Really?"

Floyd hesitated, which gave Chase a moment to think.

He used to live here, with his sister, and yet we slept in a motel? In that *motel?*

"Yep."

Something wasn't adding up.

"Does she still live here? Martinez's sister, I mean."

Floyd's eyes darted to the rearview, and Chase was surprised to see that they were moist.

"No, she d-doesn't. Martinez's sister d-d-d-d-died."

Chase looked away, suddenly feeling ashamed for being so intrusive.

"I'm sorry," she said, staring at the snow again.

"Th-th-that's okay. It happened a f-few years ago. His s-s-sister was about the s-s-s-same age as those g-girls, I think. She d-d-died after M-M-Martinez left."

Chase turned back again.

"Really?"

That would explain why he was so hard with the truck driver, with the investigation in general.

"Y-yes. It was very s-s-sad."

"I bet. I don't mean to be insensitive, Floyd, but can you tell me how she died?"

Floyd's eyes returned to the road and his voice went flat.

"She was murdered," he said, without stuttering.

For the second time since Floyd had picked her up, Chase's jaw went slack.

Murdered?

"What? How? When?"

Floyd took the off-ramp toward the airport, and turned up the circular drive. He hurried passed the rows of parked cars and stopped in front of the sign emblazoned with the Delta triangle.

"You n-n-need to hurry, Agent A-A-A-dams."

Chase, brow furrowed, wished that she had elected to start this conversation as soon as they had gotten into the car. But regardless of her curiosity, Floyd was right: if she was going to make her flight, she was going to have to haul ass.

At least I don't have any checked baggage, she thought glumly, realizing that she still hadn't received the luggage that had been lost during the first leg of her journey.

Floyd got out and hurried around to her door, but Chase opened it for herself this time.

Then she hugged the man.

The act was surprising—to both of them, really—and Floyd nearly stumbled backward.

"Thanks," she whispered in his ear. "And I have your number, I'll give you a call. Keep in touch, Floyd."

Then she left, hurrying past the dumbfounded man and into the bustling airport.

***

"Nope, still don't got it."

Chase scowled and checked her watch.

Seven minutes until the gates closed.

"Are you messing with me?" she demanded. "You told me it would be here—" Chase had to count the days in her head. "—four days ago!"

The man behind the counter raised an eyebrow.

"I told you that we were doing our best to get your stuff here from Seattle, but I have no control over that."

As frustration built inside her, Chase finally realized why there was a thick pane of glass separating the lost luggage booth from civilians.

Talk about her luggage made her feel dirty. Chase had picked up a fresh pair of undergarments from the local Winners, but she was still wearing the same jeans and shirt that she had been sporting when she had left New York nearly a week ago. Washed twice, but still…

"My gun—"

"I'm aware that your service pistol is in the missing luggage, Mrs. Adams. You've made that abundantly clear."

Yeah, and I'm going to abundantly rearrange your face, she thought with unexpected hostility.

"I'm leaving Alaska. I don't want it sent here."

The man's eyebrow rose even higher.

"If it's en route, there's nothing I—"

"I'm going to Boston. Can you send it to Boston?"

The man shrugged, then reached over and retrieved a fresh form. He put it on the counter, sliding it, along with a chewed pen, over to her side of the glass.

"If you want your luggage shipped somewhere else, you're going to have to fill out another form."

Chase grimaced and checked her watch again.

Three minutes until the gate closes.

"Can't you just copy the information from my other sheet?"

The man grabbed an apple from some hidden place beneath his desk and took a ridiculously large bite. A tiny spritz of apple juice sprayed the glass.

"Nope. Only the claimant can fill out the form."

Chase ground her teeth and then set about scribbling as quickly as she could.

And then she started to run.

"Hold it! *Hold it!* I'm coming! Don't let the plane leave! For fuck's sake, *don't let it leave!*"

PART II - Trying to Swim

ONE WEEK AGO

Chapter 25

"D<small>ID YOU ENJOY THE</small> Children's Museum?" Peter Dortmeir asked his son. When the boy didn't answer, he squeezed his hand.

"Ryder? Did you like the museum?"

The boy looked up at him with his pale blue eyes.

"I loved it," he said with a grin.

Peter laughed, and he tousled his son's hair.

"Good. Now… what's next? Lunch? You hungry?"

"Starving!"

"Alright, let's go grab something to eat then."

Peter lifted his eyes and peered along the boardwalk. It was bright and relatively warm for a March afternoon and he was forced to squint to see clearly. It was only his second time in downtown Boston, and his first at the Children's Museum, which was situated on Fort Point Channel. In the distance, he saw a small footbridge, and just beyond that he saw a yellow sign that read: GROWLING CRAB.

I could do crab… I could definitely do crab.

"Your mom ever feed you crab, Ryder?"

Ryder grunted.

"Now way. Gross. They're like underwater spiders."

Peter chuckled.

They *were* a little like underwater spiders. If spiders were absolutely succulent and delicious, which he was fairly certain they were not.

"I'm sure they have hot dogs or KD, too, if that's what you want."

"Awesome!"

With that, Ryder pulled away from him, his tiny hand slipping from Peter's palm. He darted ahead, weaving his way through several large, decorative boulders that had been placed on the boardwalk.

Peter watched him go, a smile still on his face.

How long has it been since Joelle let me have him for the entire weekend without supervision?

He wasn't sure, but it had to be three, maybe even four months. And Peter missed just holding his hand, watching the five-year-old boy run amok.

Ryder pulled himself onto one of the smaller boulders with relative ease, then leapt to another, higher stone.

Peter picked up the pace.

"Hey Ryder, why don't you get down from there?"

Ryder laughed and looked toward the tallest of the three stones, one that was at least eight feet up and three and a half feet higher than the one on which he presently stood.

When he reached for a groove in this taller rock, Peter hurried to catch up to him.

"Hey! Ryder! Get down from there, okay?"

Ryder grunted, and his mitt slipped on the snow-slickened surface. His boots were still rooted on the other stone, but he had moved onto his toes in order to stretch even further.

"Ryder!" Peter shouted, breaking into a jog. His heart started to race when he saw one of the boy's boots slip, his mitten stretching enough to reveal a thin patch of pale skin on his wrist.

Peter wrapped his arm around Ryder's knees just as his grip failed.

"Jesus, Ryder! What are you thinking?" he said in a huff as he lowered him to the ground.

A gap-toothed smile remained on his son's face.

"I'm good at climbing. Mommy says so."

Peter rolled his eyes.

"Yeah, well, I'm not Mommy, alright? You need to be more careful."

Ryder shrugged, and then immediately made his way toward the railing overlooking the channel.

"Shit," Peter grumbled as he struggled to keep up. This was turning out to be more work than he had thought.

Ryder went straight up to the railing, and hopped up onto the four-inch lip, tucking his boots between the bars as he leaned over the edge.

Peter grabbed the hood of his jacket and held tight.

"What'd I say about being more careful, Ryd—"

"What's that?"

Peter followed his son's hand.

A series of stairs led down from the boardwalk to a small platform that was cordoned off by bars. It was a landing spot for a boat, but there was no vessel moored to it. Instead, Ryder was pointing to the snow-dusted top which was covered in the smashed remains of mussels, crabs, and other random crustaceans.

Peter's smile returned; he was happy that his son was interested in these things. Despite all of the mistakes he had made over the course of the boy's short life, he had at least imbued him with a sense of curiosity.

"You hear those birds overhead? Well, they swoop down, grab a crab or mussel, and then fly way up high. Then they drop it, and the shell—"

Ryder shrugged free of Peter's grip on his jacket.

"No, not that. Mommy already told me all about that. I meant *that*."

Peter's smile became a frown.

Mother told you, huh? Well who the hell do you think told her? Hmm?

"Where?"

"Right... *there*."

Peter leaned over his son's back and saw what Ryder had been blocking with his body.

And when he did, his eyes bulged from his head and he stumbled backward.

"R—R—Ryder, get away from the railing!" Peter cried.

"Why, what is it?"

Peter grabbed his son's jacket again, and this time gave it a sharp tug.

"Hey!"

"Don't look, Ryder... whatever you do, don't look!"

Chapter 26

CHASE HALF EXPECTED THE man in the special luggage booth at Ted Stevens Anchorage International Airport to somehow be at Logan International as well, still chomping away on his damn apple, telling her that, *Whoops, sorry, your luggage was once again lost. You're going to have to fill out another form, my favorite government employee you.*

But instead, she was pleasantly surprised to be greeted by a young woman, pretty, with short brown hair, who, after seeing her badge, promptly handed over the gun that Chase had been forced to check at the other end.

"Thank you," she said, and the woman nodded and offered her a smile.

Stepping away from the booth—worried that there was still a chance that something would go wrong before she could make a clean break—Chase pulled out her phone and dialed Martinez's number.

"Agent Martinez."

"Hey, Chris, it's Chase—just landed at Logan. Is there…" she let her sentence trail off, unsure of how to broach the subject without sounding like a desperate teenager.

So you left me, and um, then you called? So, like, I'm here… what should I do next?

"I'm on the boardwalk—Fort Point Channel just outside the Children's Museum. There'll be a car waiting for you outside. Come as soon as you can."

Chase nodded as she made her way into the main airport area.

"Any—" she began, but then realized that Martinez had already hung up.

Chase shrugged and slid the phone back into her pocket. Her eyes scanned the busy airport, skipping over the hundreds of people that milled about dressed in navy suits with dark overcoats, women in long trench coats, kids wrapped in jackets that weren't that much unlike the one that she sported, the one that Martinez had so graciously given her back in Girdwood.

She was looking for Floyd, Chase realized. Maybe not him specifically, but someone like him.

Her eyes eventually fell on an elderly man leaning against a wall beside a Starbucks. In one hand, he was holding a large cup emblazoned with red snowflakes, while the other gripped a sideways iPad.

The word *ADAMS* was written in bold type across the screen.

She hurried over to him.

"Hi," she said. "I'm Agent Chase Adams."

The man nodded briskly but said nothing. It took Chase a moment to realize that he wanted to see her ID.

She took it out and showed it to him. The man scrutinized her image, then her face, then the image again for what felt like a full minute. The entire time, Chase found herself thinking that, no, this man was nothing like Floyd. She also had the feeling that it wasn't just their difference in age, either.

Eventually, the man handed it back to her.

"My name's Paul," he said curtly. "Follow me, please."

Paul... just Paul. I have to show my ID, and he gives me a single syllable.

Despite the man's age—he was pushing seventy Chase figured—he moved quickly. Paul walked so fast, in fact, that Chase had to break into a small jog just to keep up.

Chase had been right: it *was* warmer in Boston, uncharacteristically warm, in fact. With the sun shining high above her, she realized how strange time zones were. Coming from Alaska, she felt as if she had been transported to a different world. Nine hours earlier, from dreary snow and night, to maybe mid-fifties, sun high in the sky. The difference was so stark that she opened her red parka all the way.

She checked her phone, which had automatically changed to the current time zone, and realized that while she had left Alaska close to ten in the evening, it wasn't quite nine in the morning in Boston.

And yet she felt surprisingly good. She wanted to get out of her clothes and into something clean, but she didn't feel tired, at least not the way she had felt when she had first arrived in Anchorage. Sleeping on the plane had seemed to have done the trick.

"Are we—"

"Over here," Paul snapped. He led them to a battered, teal-colored sedan that was parked in a no parking zone. An airport security guard was hovering nearby, and Chase felt a knot form in her stomach.

Great, Paul's going to get his ride towed, and we're going to be stuck taking an Uber to the crime scene.

But instead, the security guard offered a subtle nod to Paul, which he returned.

Unlike Floyd, Paul didn't open her door for her, nor did she expect him to. Chase got into the front seat, and immediately crinkled her nose at the smell of stale cigarette smoke that clung to the upholstered seats.

The car squeaked when Paul got into the driver's side. To Chase's surprise, it started with a few metallic protests when he turned the key, and then they were off.

***

"How do you know Agent Chris Martinez?" Chase asked as they drove.

"Hmm?" Paul replied, without turning. His window was open a few inches, and as much as he tried to blow the cigarette smoke out the window, it kept being pushed back into the car.

Chase detested the smell but couldn't bring herself to tell this strange man to put the cigarette out. As an ex-smoker, and even when she was still smoking, she could never stand the stench of secondhand smoke. As ironic as it sounded, it made her feel ill.

"How do you know Martinez?" she asked again, swallowing her nausea.

Paul took an extended drag from his cigarette, and still avoided turning to face her.

"He worked a case in Boston about five years ago."

Chase waited for the man to elaborate, but he never did.

"And so you are… a driver? Like an—"

Finally, he turned, his small eyes boring into her.

"I'm just a friend, someone who owes Chris a favor is all."

Chase made a face.

"Alright, alright. Just trying to pass the time."

Paul brought the cigarette to his lips and turned back to the road.

Chase stared at him, the deep lines on his cheeks, the network of crow's feet at the corners of his eyes.

No, this definitely isn't Floyd.

As they continued in silence, she found her mind wandering to Brent Pine, to the dead girls, to the visions she had had when she had brushed up against Yolanda's corpse.

It dawned on Chase that if it hadn't been for her, for her comment about a van, or her interaction with Brent at the bar after she arrived when Chief Downs and Agent Martinez were in the back trying to get the proprietor to hand over the security tapes, that they never would have caught him.

Chase felt something then, something that if she didn't know herself as she did, she might have construed as pride.

But Chase knew better. It wasn't pride.

It was sadness. Deep sadness.

It took us less than a week to find Yolanda and Francine's killer, but thirty years later and Georgina's still missing.

Her arms started to itch, and she tried to think of something else. She pulled the phone from her pocket and checked for any messages.

There weren't any; none from Agent Stitts or from Brad.

"This is the channel," Paul said in a gruff voice. He tossed his cigarette out the window and then immediately lit another.

Chase turned her gaze to the window.

There were a half-dozen police cars blocking their way, and Paul was forced to come to a stop. An officer approached Paul's window, and he rolled it down a few more inches, exhaling a huge cloud of smoke into the morning air.

"You can't come through here," the police officer said, shaking his head.

"I'm—"

Agent Martinez suddenly hurried down the cobble road toward them.

"They're with me," he hollered. "Let them through."

Chapter 27

CHASE STARED AT THE reflection of the bright sun in the still water below. For a fleeting moment, she almost caught sight of her own image, but before shocking herself, she averted her eyes and looked around instead.

She had been on the boardwalk before, and remembered walking by the very location that the body had been dumped. She remembered because of the tea.

Her gaze drifted upward to the boat moored to the other side of the channel. A long rope extended off the side, the end of which was fastened to a cardboard box that floated in the water. Written on the side of the box was a single word: *TEA*.

"Already have people over there asking questions," the man who had introduced himself as Detective Tim Jasper informed her. From what Chase could gather, this man was in charge of the investigation.

Aside from Martinez and herself, of course.

What she also deduced was that Martinez and Jasper went back a ways. It was in the way they looked at each other, the way they had shaken hands and briskly nodded, instead of wasting time with perfunctory introductions.

Chase squinted across the channel.

Indeed, she could see several uniformed officers milling about on the boat.

The tea boxes, Chase knew, were symbolic of protests to the Tea Act of the late eighteenth century. Enraged by the taxes imposed on the local tea trade, and the rebates on product from the British East India Company, protesters boarded vessels and tossed their tea over the side. Now, however, it was a popular tourist destination.

"When does it open?" Chase asked, noting that there were only a handful of tourists presently on the boat.

"Nine," Detective Jasper replied.

Chase nodded and turned her attention to the body that the men in scuba gear had just managed to pull from the water. To preserve evidence, they had submerged a thick plastic sheet beneath the partially submerged corpse and had then used a winch to raise the entire contraption.

"Medical Examiner is on his way," Jasper informed her. "But judging by the paleness of her skin, I'm guessing she's been in there for a good day, day and a half, maybe. No predation, but that's likely because the water is so cold."

As Chase observed the woman—somewhere between twenty-five and thirty-five years of age, with dark hair that was pulled away from her pale face—she was reminded of a drowning that she had investigated in Central Park some six months ago.

When Senior NYPD ME, Dr. Beckett Campbell had seen the body, he had taken a particular interest in her hands.

Washerwoman hands, he had said. *It happens after the body has been submerged for twelve hours or more. You know how your fingers go all pruney if you stay in the tub for too long? Yeah, well think of washerwoman hands as an extreme version of that.*

Chase also knew that the presence of these hands was perhaps the easiest way to estimate the time of death of a submerged body. If Jasper was right, and the woman had been in the water for a day or more, her skin would be wrinkled and sloughing off, but if—

A gasp escaped her, and she whipped her head around to look at Martinez. Only Martinez wasn't staring back. Instead, he was focused on the body, his jaw clenched.

Using washerwoman hands to estimate time of death required one very obvious and specific element: hands.

And their victim didn't have any.

The woman's pale arms ended in ragged stumps. If she squinted, Chase even thought she could see gleaming ends of bones buried within the gnarled mess.

Please, please let us go. We'll do anything… anything you want.

"The boardwalk is a popular place to run in the morning," Detective Jasper said. "And if the time line is accurate, someone might have seen the body being dumped."

Chase swallowed hard again, trying her best not to jump to any conclusions about Francine and Yolanda and this poor woman.

Twenty-six-hundred miles apart… they can't be related.

Besides, they already had Brent Pine for the college murders… and as reluctant as she was to accept the fact, maybe Martinez was right; maybe he was their guy, and she had simply overestimated Brent's intelligence.

Her gut, however, told her otherwise.

I need to touch her, Chase thought with a suddenness that nearly overwhelmed her. *I need to touch the body.*

Her mouth felt incredibly dry, and any sense of alertness that she had gained during the flight from Anchorage started to leech out of her. In its place, was a duo of feelings that Chase was becoming all too familiar with as of late: lethargy and fatigue.

"Is she—" Chase began dryly, but stopped when another scuba diver suddenly surfaced, a thumb covered in thick, black gloves raised to the sky above.

Detective Jasper swore and pushed by her, and quickly headed down the stairs to the lower dock.

Martinez followed after him, but Chase stayed put and observed from above.

Three was a crowd, after all. And crowds at crime scenes almost always ended in disaster.

"What? What is it?" Jasper demanded.

The diver pulled the mask away from his mouth.

"There's another body under the boardwalk," he said. "A male—and his hands are missing too."

Chapter 28

THEY BROUGHT THE BODIES up to the main boardwalk and hastily erected white screens to keep prying eyes out and to form at least a superficial barrier for evidence collection. And while they succeeded to some degree in the latter, the former was proving more difficult. The Boston boardwalk was a popular place, it seemed, and it was near impossible to keep everyone away.

But that was Detective Jasper and Boston PD's problem. Chase had other things to worry about.

She stood inside the makeshift tent, which was already starting to warm from the sun beating down on it and opened her parka. They couldn't keep the bodies in here for long, she knew, otherwise they would start decomposing and determining an accurate time of death would become a challenge.

The ME had since arrived, a stern looking man in his seventies, and he was running some tests on the two bodies that were laid out on the thick plastic sheets that had been used to raise them from the water.

As the scuba diver had indicated, neither of the victims had hands.

"The man is Oren Vishniov," Detective Jasper stated matter-of-factly as he stepped beside Chase. "And I'm not sure, but the woman is probably his girlfriend, Julie Cooper."

Agent Martinez spoke up next.

"You know them?"

"Yeah… bunch of low level drug pushers, own a Lebanese restaurant maybe fifteen miles from here. We busted them twice last year."

"But the charges didn't stick?" Martinez followed.

Chase stepped forward, looking down at the nude corpses, at their missing hands. So far as she could tell, there was no evidence that their wounds had been cauterized, as the killer had done to Yolanda and Francine.

Nor should you expect them to be, she thought with a hint of self-loathing, *because they aren't related.*

"DA recommended suspended sentences both times."

Martinez nodded.

"Think this is drug related?"

Jasper shrugged.

"Can't rule it out."

Chase let their conversation drone on in the background while she observed the ME work. When he started swabbing the wounds on their wrists, she walked over to him and squatted.

"Were they… burned at all?" she asked.

The man turned to her, the lines on his face so deep that they resembled crinkles in folded wax paper.

"No, no evidence of burns," he replied.

"So, they died from their wounds?"

Her eyes skipped to the victims' faces as she spoke, and immediately knew that her assumption was incorrect. There was foam starting to bubble from between their pale lips. Dr. Beckett Campbell had educated her on this as well; a foam cone was a clear indication that the victims tried to breathe underwater.

"No, they drowned," the ME confirmed. "The water was so cold that when they were tossed in, all of the vessels in their wrists constricted. They would have died eventually—they were still bleeding out—but it would have taken a lot longer than on land. Best I can figure it is that they struggled to stay afloat, but without hands, they eventually slipped below the surface and drowned."

Chase grimaced.

The killer hadn't cauterized the wounds, but he didn't have to; the frigid water had done that for him.

Or her.

Chase's eyes shot up as something occurred to her.

"Why are we here?" she asked.

Martinez and Jasper, who had just wrapped up their discussion, turned to face her.

"What?" Martinez asked.

"Why are we here?" she repeated, this time softening her tone. What had been meant as an ice breaker now sounded like an accusation, even to her own ears. "I mean, two dead drug dealers? Doesn't seem to warrant the FBI's involvement."

Martinez glanced over at Jasper, who had since crossed his hands over his chest and pressed his lips together. Eventually, Martinez turned back to her.

"What do you mean?"

Chase saw anger flash in the man's eyes.

He probably sees his sister in these people, these victims.

"It's just—"

Martinez suddenly stormed over to her.

"Go get some rest, Agent Adams, you look tired," he whispered harshly.

Chase blinked, recalling that her partner had said something like this in Anchorage when she had first challenged him.

"I just—"

"Get some rest," Martinez snapped.

Chase swallowed hard, and went to push herself to her feet, when her hand accidentally grazed Oren Vishniov's thigh.

"Why are you doing this?" Oren demanded.

The man didn't answer. Instead, he continued to root through the small case at his feet, his back to them.

Julie whimpered, drawing Oren's attention. A stab of guilt filled him. His girlfriend's face was a mask of fear, her naked skin covered in goosepimples.

"I'll get us out of this, I swear," he said, but the shiver that coursed through him then made him a liar. "I'll—"

The man turned to face them, brandishing a saw in gloved hands.

"Please," Julie whimpered. "Take the drugs… we can get you more."

The man strode over to them and, as he did, Oren's and Julie's bodies swayed and rocked…

Chase's eyes snapped open.

"A boat," she whispered.

Martinez, who was now hovering over her, scowled.

"What? What are you talking about?"

"The bodies weren't thrown from the boardwalk, they were dumped out of a boat… and it was the same guy, Martinez, the same guy who killed Francine and Yolanda did this."

Chapter 29

Detective Jasper and Agent Martinez's words were muffled behind the closed window of Paul's car, but what they didn't know was that Chase was an adept lip reader.

"*What's her problem?*" Jasper asked.

Martinez stroked his chin.

"*No, no problem. She's helpful, smart.*"

"*A little fucking weird if you ask me. See the way her eyes glazed over when she accidentally touched Oren's leg? She's fucking as green as they come.*"

Martinez tilted his head to one side, and when he spoke again, Chase peered at him through the cloud of smoke that filtered from Paul's cigarette.

"*Yeah, she's pretty green.*"

And yet despite his words, Chase didn't think that her partner actually believed that. If Martinez had been at this game for, in his words, a long, *long* time, then he simply had to know better.

Chase was naive like a high-class escort was bashful.

"*And that boat business? What's that about?*"

"*I'll look into it. Hadn't really thought about it, but she could be right. I'll dig into the logs from the fishing boats, rentals, etc. Have your guys do the same.*"

Martinez's face suddenly broke into a grin and he slapped the Detective on the back.

"*We'll help you solve this one, Tim,*" he said. "*We've got your back.*"

Something flickered across Jasper's eyes, something dark and unexpected.

"*You owe me,*" the detective said. He spoke so quietly that his words were completely inaudible from inside the vehicle.

Martinez offered a simple nod as a reply. After a short pause, Jasper's expression lightened.

"Meet for a beer later?"

Martinez smiled.

"Mind if I bring the greenhorn?"

Jasper shrugged.

"Sure, it'll be fun. At the Anchor, like old times? How about ten?"

"Perfect. That'll give me time to catch up on some sleep." Martinez's smile grew, and he slapped Jasper on the back a second time. *"See you then, Timmy. Maybe you should get some sleep, too. You look like you've got one foot in the grave."*

With that, Martinez slid away from the detective and approached the car. Paul rolled down the window.

"Hey, Paul, thanks for taking Agent Adams around," Martinez said, his face stern again.

Paul took a drag of his cigarette.

"Sure, no problem."

Martinez raised his eyes to Chase, but when he spoke, his words were directed at Paul again.

"Can you take Agent Adams to get some fresh clothes? Something to wear? Luggage was misplaced somewhere in the Pacific Northwest."

Paul grunted, and Chase detected a hint of a smile on his lips.

"Sure."

Then to Chase, Martinez added, "You'll be happy to know that we've got nicer digs here in Beantown... I know the owner of the *W Hotel*. We'll be staying there."

Just the mention of the *W Hotel* and the idea of a giant, king-size bed covered in dozens of plush pillows, was enough to make Chase's eyes droop.

Besides, anything would be better than *Girdwood Motel*.

"Sounds good," she said with a tired smile.

Martinez placed both hands on the partially opened window.

"And be ready for ten, we're going for drinks with Jasper."

The man straightened, and then backed away from the car.

"Oh, and Paul?"

Chase's driver looked up with red-rimmed eyes.

"Yeah?"

"Put out the damn cigarette. That shit'll kill you."

***

Chase wasn't one for shopping, never had been, so she managed to make it in and out of a Winners in under ten minutes armed with a handful of undergarments, three tops, and two pairs of pants. She also purchased a hat, a scarf, and some gloves, but kept the red coat that Martinez had loaned her.

It wasn't the money—she had enough of that from her online poker days—but there was something about the jacket that offered her a modicum of comfort, of consistency.

She had been zipping around the country over the past week, racking up the air miles without any idea of how long this whole ordeal was going to last.

Surely, this couldn't be all there was to the FBI, could it? There had to be some down time, a day or two to catch her breath, to discuss the cases that they formulated then fled before they could see them through.

All she knew was that Agent Martinez had told her to get up, pack her bags—a lot of good that had done—and head to the airport.

Chase yawned as she approached Paul's sedan.

A good... afternoon... nap, that's all I need to collect myself. To think clearly again.

Paul had put out his cigarette when Agent Martinez had asked but had lit up another... and another... the moment they had hit the road.

Chase stashed the bags in the backseat and then got into the front.

"Where to next, boss?" Paul said, a fresh cigarette dangling from between his lips.

Boss... that's what Drake used to call me.

A strange wave of nostalgia washed over her. Things hadn't gone smoothly in New York, but at least they had followed a reasonable pattern, something that she could understand.

Chase shook her head and yawned again.

"Yeah, take me to the hotel, Paul. I need to get some rest."

Chapter 30

"Come on, Georgina. Let's go. Mom'll be waiting," Chase said.

The man in the van smirked, pulling his large aviator sunglasses down his nose.

"You're going to regret it," the man said, leaning out of the window of his van and peering up at the bright sun. "It's only going to get hotter."

Chase moved closer to her sister, putting her body between the young girl and the car.

"We're fine."

"You don't look fine; you guys look hot. Come on, I'll give you a lift. I won't bite, promise," the man held up crossed fingers as he spoke. "This is your last chance."

Something chimed inside Chase's head then. It wasn't *what* the man said, per se, but *how* he said. And despite this realization, she wasn't actually sure what it was that had activated the alarm bells.

And yet they were blaring—blaring long and loud.

"Come on, let's go," she hissed at her sister.

But Georgina didn't go; instead, she slid toward the car.

"But it's soooo hot," she whined. "Let's just—"

Chase's eyes narrowed.

"Let's go."

"No, I—"

"Georgina—Now."

Behind her sister, Chase heard a car door open.

She reached for Georgina then, tried to grab her hand.

Only, to her horror, she realized that her little sister, her five-year-old sister, didn't have any hands. She had arms, small, thin arms, but where her hands should have been were only ragged stumps.

"*Georgina!*" *she screamed.*

Someone was laughing, Chase realized.

The man in the aviator sunglasses stepped out of the van. Only now he wasn't just a large man, but huge, a massive shadow that grew until he blacked out the sun.

"*Run, Georgie! Run!*" *Chase screamed.*

Her sister's body suddenly went limp, and Georgina looked down at her own legs.

"*I can't,*" *she whispered.*

Chase followed her gaze and realized why.

Like her arms, Georgina's legs ended too soon.

Her feet were gone, sawed off by the same crude tool that had been used to remove her hands.

Georgina looked up at her, tears in her eyes.

"*Don't leave me,*" *her sister whispered.* "*Please, Chase, don't leave me.*"

Chase screamed.

Then she turned and ran.

Chapter 31

CHASE AWOKE DRENCHED IN sweat. Her pillow, one of many, once a fluffy, down-filled, eighty-dollar affair, was sagging from the weight of her perspiration.

Momentarily disoriented, she blinked rapidly, trying to force her eyes to focus. Every time they closed, even for a split second, she saw her sister's face, her cute, button nose, her wide green eyes.

And the man in the aviator shades was looming behind her.

"Shit," she swore.

Her body ached, but she managed to pull herself to a seated position, scratching absently at the insides of her elbows.

It had been a long, long week, week and a half. And it had finally taken its toll on her.

Chase sighed and stretched her legs.

One thing was for certain: the *W Hotel* was a fine sight better than the roach motel she had crashed in in Anchorage.

With a groan, Chase stood and checked the digital clock on the night table.

Then she swore again.

It was almost nine in the evening; somehow, despite her nightmares, she had managed to sleep all day.

Chase rubbed the last vestiges of sleep from her eyes and when she pulled her fists away, she found herself staring at the stainless steel mini fridge embedded across from her bed.

One hour… one hour until I have to meet Martinez and Jasper.

Chase stood and made her way to the fridge. She opened it, but instead of reaching inside, she first let the cool air wash over her damp, sweaty skin. Clad only in bra and underwear, she pulled out the first thing that her clammy fingers touched: a bottle of Modelo.

She glanced at the gold paper covering the top, decided that it was too much work, and went for a bottle of Budweiser instead.

The beer went down smooth and quick, and in three chugs, she had finished it.

Like the cold air from the still-open fridge, the beer felt great in her stomach. In fact, it felt so good that she immediately reached for another.

After finishing her second beer, in twice as many gulps this time, Chase hopped into the shower and scraped the sweat from her skin.

The water caused her hair to form clumps in front of her face, and an image of Francine's frozen hair, her eyes white, mouth open, flashed in her mind.

Chase shook her head and quickly finished washing up.

"Why are these cases fucking with my head?" she said out loud as she stepped from the shower.

And why are memories of Georgina coming back so strongly?

Her sister was never far from her mind, nor was what had happened that day. But after nearly thirty years, things had a way of slipping into the background. Never quite gone, but...

And now they were back and as vivid as they had ever been.

The inside of her arms started to itch, and Chase scratched furiously at the small dots that forever marked her flesh.

A half-chewed nail broke the skin and she winced.

Cursing, Chase dabbed at the blood with a piece of toilet paper.

Serves you right.

After toweling off, she headed back to the bedroom. Chase went to the fridge first to grab another beer, and then turned on the radio.

Ironically, it was a Drake tune: *Hotline Bling*. She chuckled to herself and took a swig of beer.

Then she turned the music up loud and swayed to the beat as she started to dress.

***

"There she is!" Agent Martinez hollered, raising his glass. "And look at that, only half an hour late."

Chase smirked and walked over to the booth in which Agent Martinez and Detective Jasper sat. Both men were dressed in matching blue sweaters and jeans. If it weren't for their very different faces—Martinez was handsome with tanned skin, whereas Jasper had bold features and skin the consistency and texture of stewed oatmeal—Chase might have thought them the Bobbsey Twins.

"Two for one sale?" she said as she took the seat across from Martinez.

Jasper threw his head back and laughed.

She saw his tonsils then, and knew that like her, the glass in front of him was far from his first; his demeanor couldn't be more different than it had been earlier in the day at the boardwalk.

"What's a lady gotta do to get a drink around here?" she said.

Martinez held up a hand.

"Hey! Let's get—" he turned to her. "What do you drink? You look like a beer type of girl to me."

Chase raspberried her lips.

"Beer'll do."

"Alrighty then. Let's get this woman a beer!"

***

Anchor Bar was relatively quiet, which wasn't surprising for a Tuesday in March, and the two FBI Agents and the Boston PD Detective were its only patrons as p.m. bled into a.m.

Over the course of the evening, Detective Jasper's skin had gone from pasty to beet red, a shade that darkened with every subsequent beverage. His words had also gone from crisp, abrupt sentences to ones that lacked punctuation and maybe even spaces.

Chase noticed this, but not overtly. She too was feeling the effects of the alcohol and, her senses, in addition to her inhibitions, had been numbed.

"Goddamn musta been hard to swim without flippers," Jasper said with a chuckle. Chase could tell the man had meant it as a joke, but it was in such poor taste that even in her inebriated state she couldn't help but cringe.

"And that, *gggentlemen*, *'s'my* key to leave," she slurred, pounding back the last of her beer. She went to stand but teetered and Martinez put a hand on her arm.

Chase smiled wanly.

"Thanks."

"Sure," he said, also rising. At some point during the evening, he had rolled up his sleeves and now that he was steadying her, Chase saw a strange tattoo that ran the length of his forearm. It was simply drawn, without shading: an outline of a snake devouring an eyeball.

What a strange tattoo, she thought absently.

"You know what? We're both staying at the same hotel. Why don't we just cab together?"

"So long as the Agency picks up the tab, doesn't bother me at all," Chase replied.

"I'll see you in the morning, Jasper," Martinez said with a nod in the red-faced man's direction. "We'll visit Vishniov's store, see if there's anything there. Let's wrap this one up and move on to the next."

"Sounds good. My men've already been through th'place, but it'll be good to get another set of eyes," Jasper slurred. "Fuckin' drug pushers, lowlife scum. Got what they deserved, maybe."

Chase squinted at the man. Martinez also shot him a queer look, and was about to turn and leave, when Jasper's hand shot out and grabbed Martinez by the forearm.

Martinez glanced at the man's hand briefly before shrugging him off. Then in a move that seemed to Chase to fall just short of being casual, her partner pulled his sleeve down and covered the tattoo.

Jasper tilted his head, indicating for Martinez to move closer, then offered a not so subtle look in Chase's direction.

Chase politely looked away but perked her ears.

She couldn't help it.

"So, Chris, how you doin'? You know, after what happened to Anna? Things still—"

Martinez said nothing but shot Jasper such a look that the man visibly recoiled.

Then Chase's partner smiled and patted Jasper gently on the shoulder.

"See you tomorrow, Jasper. Sleep it off, man."

Chapter 32

CHASE HAD MANAGED TO hold it together fairly well at the bar, but once outside the Anchor, things immediately started to deteriorate. Alcohol wasn't foreign to her—Martinez was right, she *was* a beer girl—but she usually limited herself to two or three.

Not seven, like she had imbibed tonight. That, and her irregular, broken sleep pattern had made for a toxic combination.

Inside the cab, her vision started to swim, and she was forced to open the window; the shock of the rushing air kept her grounded.

The good thing was, Chase was drunk enough not to think about… anything, really.

Except for the sweet taste of beer on her palate.

Martinez was predictably silent during the ride, which was fine by her. She suspected by the way that his head dipped periodically that he was drunker than he was letting on too, and that was fine.

Maybe it would serve to loosen him up a little.

The cab pulled up to the *W*, and Martinez reached into his wallet. He pulled out a twenty and handed it to the driver.

"You gonna be alright, miss?" the driver asked, lifting his eyes to the rearview.

Chase smirked.

"I'll be fine," she bit her lip. "And keep the change."

The air was cold, and it was sharp in her nose as she inhaled. In the car, it had seemed mild out, what with the wind whipping in from the crack in the window. But outside, it seemed as cold as it had in Anchorage, despite her alcohol consumption.

Chase shivered and hurried to catch up with Martinez, who had already started toward the entrance.

The doorman gave her a look as they passed, his expression similar to the one that the cab driver had given her, but thankfully the man fell short of asking if she was okay.

What is it with this world that every man thinks that it's their job to protect me? As if every woman is a victim?

It seemed like Martinez was the only man who hadn't asked if she was okay, if she was fine, alright, good, perfect, if she needed something, wanted something, desired for *anything*.

The irony was that Chase wasn't okay; she hadn't been okay for some time now. And yet she got by. She got by and solved murders, put bad people under the watch of slightly better people, and she was good at it.

Like Brent Pine... I got him, I got justice for those poor girls...

The elevator ride and subsequent walk to her room were a blur, and before she knew it, she was outside her door.

Chase glanced over at Martinez, who had the room next to her.

"Goodnight, Chris," she said softly.

The man stared directly into her eyes.

"Goodnight, Chase. I'll see you in the morning."

Even though he hadn't asked if she was okay, he was gentlemen enough to watch as she struggled with her keycard before finally getting the lock to disengage.

"Goodnight," she said again, although this time the words were more for herself than for Martinez's benefit.

With a deep breath, she entered the room and closed the door. Then she pressed her back against it from the inside.

Shutting her eyes, she waited for the visions to come.

They took a while, but eventually they showed up, intoxicated or not.

First, of Georgina, then of the man with the aviator shades.

Then the girls… the dead girls with the missing limbs.

The syringe.

The reek of sweat.

"Fuck," she whispered.

When are they going to leave me alone? When is Georgina finally going to let me move on?

But she knew the answer to that question. Georgina would never let her go, not until Chase found her.

And found the man responsible.

A single tear traced a line down her cheek, and she swiped at it awkwardly with the back of a trembling hand.

With her other, she slipped it into her purse and pulled out her cell phone.

She didn't want to be alone tonight. Tonight, she wanted to hear someone's voice, someone she loved.

When Chase saw that Brad hadn't called, that she had no missed messages, she unexpectedly started to sob.

"I don't want to be alone," she whispered. "I don't want to be alone tonight."

Chase dialed Brad's number, but there was no answer.

"Where are you? Why don't you answer my calls? Why don't you pick up the fucking phone?"

Drunk or not, she was smart enough not to leave a message. Chase hung up then dialed Agent Stitts's number.

Her whole life she had wanted to be an FBI Agent, and now that she had achieved this goal, she realized that this had done nothing to satisfy her needs.

Because Georgina was still out there… somewhere.

Stitts didn't answer either, and Chase took a deep, shuddering breath. She wiped the tears from her eyes and then made a decision.

She didn't want to be alone tonight, not with her thoughts, with her strange visions, her memories.

Chase clenched her jaw and pulled away from the door. She opened it and then walked to the room next to hers.

She knocked once and waited.

Several seconds passed before a shirtless Martinez pulled the door wide.

Chase lowered her eyes, and then she stepped inside.

Chapter 33

CHASE SHIVERED HERSELF AWAKE. She blinked twice, then pulled the sheet up over her naked body, tucking it tightly beneath her chin.

Then she looked around.

Martinez was sitting on a chair in the corner of the room, his bare back to her. She saw some papers on the table, including what looked like a ticket stub and receipt from his flight from Anchorage to Boston. Martinez was fiddling with something in his lap, but she couldn't make out what it was.

"I'm sorry about your sister," Chase said, unsure of what had prompted the words.

Had I been dreaming? Dreaming about Georgina?

Martinez froze.

"Go back to sleep, Chase. We have a busy day tomorrow," he said over his shoulder.

Chase closed her eyes, and sleep took her again.

Chapter 34

THE CELL PHONE ALARM, a piercing jingle, sounded like the soundtrack to a nightmare.

Chase awoke with a start, her head spinning, her tongue thick with the sickly-sweet taste of fermented alcohol.

Bile rose in her throat, and she leapt to her feet, barely noticing that she was completely nude.

She made it to the bathroom, but not to the toilet. Holding her hair back with one hand, she puked into the sink.

Hot, sour liquid splashed the porcelain, and the sight of the greenish-brown substance inspired another bout of vomit.

After voiding her stomach of its contents and adding a few desperate dry heaves just to be sure, Chase splashed ice cold water on her face. Then she pulled the sallow skin below her eyes down with her fingertips, noting that the edges were tinged pink.

A quick glance around only served to further disorient her. It *looked* like her room, seemed almost exactly like her room, in fact, only it wasn't; it was different.

It took her a few moments to figure it out: it was a mirror image of her room.

And with this realization, memories of the previous night came roaring back.

"No," she moaned. If she needed further proof, she spotted a used condom hanging over the edge of the plastic wastebasket. "Fuck."

Chase slammed her hands down against the basin and instantly regretted it. The sound sent a blistering shard through her skull.

What have I done? What the hell have I done?

But she knew what she had done.

"Martinez?" she said softly.

No answer.

Chase pulled away from the sink and leaned back into the room.

It was empty and for this, she was grateful.

Chase hurried to dress, and then grabbed her cell phone and sat on the side of the bed. She didn't even remember bringing it last night.

Instinctively scrolling to her husband's name, Chase hesitated before making the call.

Even though she doubted that Brad would answer, she didn't trust herself in her present state to not leave a message that would only come back to haunt her later.

Still in a daze, she looked about the room. Not only was Martinez not there, but it appeared as if the man had taken most of his belongings with him when he'd left. Everything, in fact, except for a single sheet of paper lying in the center of the table Chase had awoken to him sitting at in the middle of the night.

It read, simply: *210 Ashburn Road—Oren's restaurant. Paul will take you there. M.*

Chase allowed herself a final moment of self pity, and then did what she always did when things went south.

She buried herself in her work.

***

Paul's sedan was waiting outside the *W*, just as Martinez had written it would be. The man leaned out the window as she approached and waved her over. He was chain-smoking and didn't bother hiding this fact from her.

Chase got into the passenger seat and took a sip of the scalding coffee she had poured herself in the lobby. After her vomiting session, most of her hangover had subsided, leaving her with just an odd, lightheaded feeling.

"Rough night?" Paul asked with a smirk.

Chase ignored the comment.

"Take me to two hundred ten Ashburn," she said.

Paul put the car into drive.

"Yes, ma'am," he replied, his voice dripping with sarcasm.

Regardless of what had happened the night before, she still had a killer to catch.

And this was, and always would be, Chase Adams's priority.

Chapter 35

IF OREN VISHNIOV'S JOINT was a five-star restaurant, then *Girdwood Motel* was the Taj Mahal. Situated in the back of a warehouse, the nondescript building was rundown, bordering on derelict. The brick exterior was worn and covered in graffiti, and the service desk, a crude opening cut out of the wall, was filthy.

Paul pulled his car behind Martinez's rental and what she assumed was Detective Jasper's unmarked police vehicle.

The glass door beside the service desk was propped open, and, as Chase approached, she realized that the top pane of glass had been smashed.

She announced her presence, and both Martinez and Jasper turned to face her.

"Morning," Martinez offered. Jasper grumbled the same.

Whatever joviality and friendliness that had fallen over them the night prior in the pub had clearly been expended. Martinez, for one, turned away immediately after saying hello. Chase thought she picked up a smirk on Jasper's pale face, but she knew enough not to mistaken this for kindness.

Fuck it, she thought. *Who cares if Martinez told Jasper about what happened last night?*

Chase recalled what she had instructed the New York public to do when there was a murderer on the loose targeting women.

Be a bitch—no one gets taken advantage of if they act like a bitch. There are easier targets out there than a woman with attitude.

She would not succumb to the idea, the trope, that she had to be the damsel in distress, the nice, doting girl.

And Chase definitely wouldn't be embarrassed for sleeping with Martinez. What did it say about society when a man could be proud of his sexual exploits, while the only expectation for the woman was that she should be reserved and bashful. Why was it assumed that the man had *won* her, implying that she had somehow lost in the exchange?

As much as she regretted the decision—for Brad, not for the act itself—she had had a good time. And she wasn't going to be ashamed of it.

Fuck it.

"What've you found?" she asked as she strode forward, chin held high. "Break-in?"

Jasper squinted at her, but only for a moment, and then his voice took on a professional tone.

"Looks that way," he gestured to the door that she had just passed through. "Glass is broken, the register's been smashed. What I think, though, is that this is what they were after."

Jasper pulled a pen from his pocket and used it to lift a clear plastic bag roughly the size of a change purse. It was mostly empty, but even from where she stood, Chase could see a small amount of white powder clinging to one of the interior corners. There was also a design of sorts on the front of the plastic, but it had been sliced through, obscuring the image.

Chase nodded and tried to piece together the scene.

Desperate junkies come by after the shawarma house closed, beg Oren for his dope, maybe ask him for some on credit. Oren refuses, and the junkie, or junkies, smash the window and gain entrance. They overtake the man and his wife, grab the dope, and flee.

… and then the junkie forces Oren and Julie into a boat, takes them to the channel, chops off their hands, and throws them in.

She shook her head.

The narrative didn't work at all.

"We should get CSU in here—"

"Any blood on the scene?" Chase interrupted Jasper.

The man pressed his lips together tightly.

"No. Not that I can see."

Martinez took the plastic from Jasper's pen and put it into an evidence bag.

"What do you think happened here, Chase?" he asked.

Chase looked around again.

Her eyes eventually fell on the smashed pane of glass. It was hard to tell but, judging by the size of the jagged pieces that still hung to the frame, it looked as if the point of impact was at about eye-level for her, about eighteen-inches above the lock.

She took several steps forward and observed the cash register next. It was, as Jasper had told her, lying on the floor. The drawer was open and empty, and the corner was dented.

"Chase?" Martinez asked, an eyebrow raised.

Chase ignored him and continued to observe her surroundings. To the right were two vertical spits that still held a couple of pounds of either chicken or beef, but the element behind them had been turned off. The vegetables in the tray tucked safely behind the sneeze guard still looked fresh.

Chase lifted her eyes past Jasper and Agent Martinez, to a door that hung ajar. Although she couldn't get the best view of what was inside, its presence was enough for things to start to fall into place.

"I think this was staged," she said simply. "I think it was staged to look like a robbery, but none of it makes sense."

Jasper rose to his feet.

"Hold on now. Oren Vishniov and his partner Julie Cooper are known dealers, and when junkies—"

Chase shook her head.

"No junkie did this."

Jasper's frown became a scowl.

"This is bullshit, Martinez. This chick comes in here—"

Martinez hushed him and held up a finger.

"Let her finish."

"Bullshit, Martinez. You guys were called into help, and now—"

"Let her finish," Martinez repeated with more authority this time.

Jasper's mouth snapped shut, and Chase eyed both men suspiciously.

What the hell is going on here? Aren't we all supposed to be on the same side? Aren't we supposed to be collaborating, not fighting with each other? What the—

"Go on, Chase," Martinez said, his tone softening, "tell us what you think."

Chase cleared her throat.

"Like I said, I think this was staged. The door... look where it was smashed—it's too high. Anyone who wants to break into this place would smash the glass right near the lock, not in the middle of the pane. And the empty bag of dope? What junkie in their right mind would leave that here, in the middle of the room?"

Chase's heart skipped a beat, and she fought images of her past, of trying to heat the spoon, to melt the heroin, all the while her hands shaking so badly that she could barely hold it.

"A junkie would take that bag, flip it inside out, and lick the plastic if they have to, just to get every last morsel of powder."

Chase stepped forward.

"Oren and his wife, or partner or whatever, were known drug dealers, right?"

Jasper didn't respond, but Martinez nodded. She stepped by the men and made her way to the door at the back of the room. A passing glance and her suspicions were confirmed; although it had initially been designed as a store room, it had been re-purposed for more illicit activities.

"This room here… the door's reinforced. Whatever Oren was, he was prepared. You're telling me that not only did Oren not make it to the safe room, but his wife didn't either? Shit, I wouldn't be surprised if you found weapons in there… it'd be the first place they'd go if someone broke in."

"Oren was a lot of things, but he wasn't a violent man," Jasper said.

Chase shrugged.

"Still… someone in his business would have some sort of protection. But instead of running into the safe room, they came out here, in the open, when a junkie allegedly smashed the window. Doesn't make sense."

"Well then, Professor X, what *did* happen here?" Jasper asked.

Chase paused, and for the first time since starting her dissertation, she looked down.

But only for a moment; she raised her eyes and leveled them at Martinez.

"Like I said, I think this was staged. And I also think our killer is the same one as in Alaska."

Chapter 36

"Yeah, nice theory, but I like mine better," Jasper remarked with a scowl.

Chase's eyes narrowed.

"And what's that?"

"What's *what*?" Jasper snapped.

"Your theory—what do *you* think happened here?"

Jasper turned to Martinez for support, but the man simply shrugged, silent encouragement to go ahead and offer his own opinion. To top off the strangeness, it appeared to Chase that Martinez was smirking, that he might actually be enjoying this.

Chase wasn't in the mood; she still felt lightheaded, and the nausea was starting to return.

What are we doing here, anyway? If Martinez thinks that this is just a run-of-the-mill junkie-fueled murder, why is the FBI here? Another 'favor?'

"What I think? What does it matter what I think when we have the truth-seer here? And what the hell happened in Alaska? Martinez, I thought you told me that everything got wrapped up?"

The smile slid off Martinez's face.

"It is."

Detective Jasper threw his hands up and he whipped around to face Chase again.

"Fine, you want to know what I think? I think that one of Oren's customers came by a few nights ago needing a fix. One of his regulars who doesn't raise an alarm, but when Oren asks him to pay for his goddamn shawarma and baggie of heroin, the man refuses. Or maybe he pretends like he's going to pay, but instead smashes the window. Then he comes in here—maybe with a couple of his junkie buddies in tow—and they grab Oren and Julie and tie them up. They take what drugs they have, then drag the two of them out to the channel all hopped up on God knows what. They demand more drugs and Oren either refuses, or, being the small-time prick that he was, he simply doesn't have any more. They chop off his and his girlfriend's hands and toss them overboard." Jasper wiped his hands together, a strange gesture given the context. "Seen it before, and I'll see it again. I've got my men out there right now, shaking down some of Oren's regulars. I guarantee they find something on one of them, or, better yet, I'll bet one of them cracks."

Jasper finished with an air of smugness, but while the theory was garbage, Chase found herself agreeing with the last part of his statement.

They *would* find something on one of the junkies, but that didn't mean that they committed the crime. It was only a feeling in the pit of her stomach, a little flutter beside the knot that was there from not believing that the charming bartender, Brent Pine, had killed Yolanda and Francine, but she couldn't ignore it.

Not anymore.

Chase scrunched her nose and then blurted, "That's not what you think happened, Jasper... that's what you *want* to have happened. There's a big difference."

Jasper gawked.

"You know what? I don't need this fucking lecture from a greenhorn broad."

Martinez opened his mouth, but Jasper continued before the man could get a word in edgewise.

"No, screw this, Martinez. I didn't ask for you guys to come here, and I definitely don't need your fucking conspiracy serial killer theories messing up my investigation."

"Tim—"

"No, seriously, Chris, this is it. I'm not raising a serial killer flag because a couple of drug dealers were murdered. Shit, this is almost a daily occurrence in my jurisdiction."

Now it was Martinez's turn to raise his hands.

"Alright, alright, just calm down, Jasper. I'm sorry we couldn't be of any help here. And I'm sure you're right about what happened. Chase sometimes just… well, just gets carried away."

Jasper grunted and was about to add something else, when the radio on his shoulder crackled.

"Detective Jasper?"

Jasper turned his back to Chase, who was still reeling over the way that Martinez had thrown her under the bus and clicked the talk button.

"Yeah?" he snapped.

"It's Lieutenant Danvers."

"What do you want, Danvers? I'm kind of busy here."

"Well, we found one of Oren's junkies on Washburn St., and you're not going to believe this, but he's actually wearing Oren's watch."

Jasper spun around, a sinister leer on his lips.

"What do you mean, his watch? How do you know it's Oren's watch?"

"Well, because it's inscribed with O. Vishniov on the back. I don't think there are too many—"

"Danvers, you still at Washburn St.?"

"Yeah, we've got the junkie in the back of the car."

"Okay, sit tight. I'm only about fifteen minutes from there. I don't want anyone to speak to him until I arrive, got it?"

"Ten-four."

Jasper's hand fell away from the radio.

"What'd I say?" he remarked with a grin.

It was Chase who wanted to say something. No, not say — *scream*. She wanted to scream that there was something going on here, that this wasn't right, but a feeling in her gut told her that chiming in now would do more harm than good.

Chase bit her tongue to prevent from speaking.

"Looks like this is going to wrap up nicely, like I fucking said it would," Jasper continued, his words so dripping with condescension that Chase was surprised he wasn't drooling. "I'll get CSU in here to comb the scene, but it looks like everything is falling into place. It was nice to see you, Chris."

He stepped forward and shook Agent Martinez's hand quickly, and then walked by Chase. She had to step out of the way to avoid being bumped.

When he was gone, Chase turned to Martinez.

"What the hell was that all about?"

Martinez sighed.

"I told you before, in Alaska; this job is as much about people management as it is solving crimes. These guys... the older guard, they don't like agents coming in and trying to run the show."

Martinez moved toward her, and together they started toward the door.

"It just requires a little tact, is all. You have to ease them away from their theories toward what you think is more accurate. It's kind of like a Chinese finger trap: if you pull too hard, it only makes things worse."

"But—" *this is nuts,* Chase wanted to say.

Martinez cut her off.

"But... that's just the way things go, Chase. You'll learn. Like I said, I've been at this a long time."

Chase looked at him then, trying to gauge if he, like Detective Jasper and Chief Downs before him, was patronizing her.

After a moment of consideration, she decided that he wasn't.

Just a poor choice of words, perhaps.

"But... a junkie? Really?" Chase said at last. "You can't really believe that... a junkie chopping off hands and tossing bodies into the canal."

Martinez shrugged, and then zipped his jacket to the top as they stepped outside.

"Maybe... probably not. But we can't rule out that one of Oren's competitors did this to him—who knows, maybe he was late on moving money back up the chain? The point is, we caught the guy in Anchorage, and whatever the reason why Oren and Julie were hacked up, there's no serial killer on the loose here. You need to let it go, Chase. Not everything comes together like a perfect jigsaw puzzle."

The finality in Martinez's tone made it clear that the conversation was closed, and despite having more to say, Chase got that feeling again; the feeling that it was best to keep her mouth shut.

"What now?" she settled on.

Martinez looked at her and raised an eyebrow.

"Now? Now I go back to the hotel and get some rest. Didn't sleep much last night."

Chapter 37

CHASE COLLAPSED ONTO HER bed and closed her eyes. Then she kicked off her shoes and pinched the bridge of her nose.

The feeling of light-headedness was mostly gone, and although she still had the sweet taste of beer on her tongue, any other remnants of a hangover had receded into the background. Unlike Martinez, however, Chase wasn't tired. Quite the contrary, actually.

She was wired. Wired because none of what had happened made sense. Not her time in Alaska, not Jasper's explosion in Oren's shawarma shop, nothing.

In fact, nothing really made sense since the morning when she had received Martinez's call.

For instance, who did they report to? Who was their superior? What happens with her opinions on Oren and Julie's murders?

Both Jasper and Martinez had told her to leave it alone, and the fact that the FBI wasn't here on official business meant that she… what? Couldn't file a report? Couldn't write down her thoughts or opinions? What the fuck did it all mean?

Before meeting Agent Stitts, she had thought that the FBI was one of the more structured, regimented branches of the government. Stitts had changed that, what with his personal approach to her and the crimes he studied, his reliance on things like gut instinct that weren't part of the normal police vernacular let alone practice.

What's your gut telling you, Chase? Millions of years of evolution have generated safeguard measures for ensuring that you recognize the signs, even if your mind is preoccupied. You've got more neurons in your gut than a dog has in his brain, and we all know how they can smell fear. So trust it, Chase. Do yourself a favor and trust your gut feeling, your instincts.

The words in her head came in Stitts's voice, and it was so startling that Chase had to open her eyes to make sure that he wasn't actually in the room with her.

He wasn't.

Chase reached into her pocket and pulled out her cell phone. For the first time since she had been awoken by Martinez's call, she hoped that Brad *hadn't* called her.

Because this time she wouldn't know what to say to him, if she could lie if put to the question.

If she could tell him again that she was alright, that it wasn't like in Seattle, that she wasn't so engrossed in her work that she could keep her head straight and above water.

But he hadn't called, so Chase dialed Stitts's number instead.

"You've reached the mailbox of Jeremy Stitts. If this is an emergency, please call the FBI directly. Otherwise, leave me a message and I'll get back to you."

A robotic voice followed, informing her of what she already knew: that Stitts's mailbox was full.

Chase shook her head and tossed the phone on the bed beside her.

Use your gut, Stitts's voice echoed in her head. *What's it telling you, Chase?*

Her gut was telling her that she was hungry, that it was nearly noon and she had yet to eat today. But it was also telling her that the murders in Alaska and here in Boston were connected, regardless of what Martinez and the others said.

How, why, when, what... these questions still eluded her, but it was a start, at least.

"Fuck it," Chase said out loud. Without Agent Stitts, and no idea who else to contact, she had no choice but to confront Martinez again, no matter how uncomfortable it was going to be.

With a groan, Chase rose off the bed, slid her cell phone into her pocket, and started toward the door. Remembering what had happened the night prior, however, Chase made a detour before heading to the door.

In order to avoid giving the wrong impression or, God forbid, a repeat, Chase put her red parka back on and zipped it up tight.

With a deep breath, she pulled the door open and stepped into the hallway. She counted six steps from her door to Martinez's. Her knuckles rapped loudly off the wood.

Immediately, Chase heard stirring from inside the room. Half expecting a groggy Martinez to answer given what he had said about his fatigue, she prepared a mental apology.

She was surprised, however, that when the door opened, Martinez was fully dressed and looked alert.

"Chase? What can I do for you?" he asked tentatively.

Clearly, the man was also regretting what had happened the night before.

"I just want to talk," Chase said quietly. Martinez nodded, smiled, and opened the door wide.

Chase was about to enter when the phone in her pocket buzzed.

Is it Stitts finally getting back to me, or is it Brad?

She resisted the urge to look and instead returned Martinez's half-baked smile, fearing that hers was as fake as it felt.

"I just want to talk," she reiterated as she stepped inside.

Chapter 38

"I'M JUST... I'M JUST confused. I mean, I don't know what to do. I don't think that a desperate junkie chopped off Oren and his wife's hands any more than I think the charming bartender removed Yolanda and Francine's feet. Something's not adding up—I'm almost positive that whoever did these horrible things, it was the same person, the same killer. I don't know how or why, or what the connection is between the two besides drugs, but I'm sure of it. And, look, I know you don't want to hear it, but Martinez..." Chase looked down at her hands. "You know how you said that you've been at this for a long time? While I might be new to the Agency, I'm not new to this... to murder, to *pain*. And I know that you said that things aren't necessarily going to be wrapped up in a pretty little bow, that things don't always connect or even make sense. But in this case... in these cases, they're related—I just know it."

Martinez stared at her for so long that she began to shift uncomfortably on the corner of the bed.

Was it a mistake coming to him?

But the damage, if there was any, had already been done. She said her piece.

In fact, *her* damage had happened long ago.

"Don't you want a ride, girls? I mean, it's really hot out there. Really hot. And I have air conditioning. I bet you can even feel it from the sidewalk. What d'you say?"

"Stitts really did get to you, didn't he? Shit, he tried the same with me. Sometimes it works, sometimes it doesn't, I guess," Martinez said softly.

Chase's brow furrowed.

"What do—"

Martinez smiled and then clapped his hands together. The sound was so loud and unexpected that Chase jumped a little.

"I need a drink," he exclaimed.

Chase's brow furrowed, and it took her a moment to regain her composure. She hadn't intended to offer such an outward display of emotion and was usually good at keeping these sorts of things close to her chest from playing poker, but Martinez's response caught her completely off guard.

Even considering last night, he didn't strike her as a man who drank in the middle of the day.

"Normally, I don't do this," Martinez said, as if reading her mind. With that, he stood and turned away from her, making his way toward the bathroom where the minibar was located. He ducked out of sight and continued. "But this has been a messed-up day, wouldn't you agree? And it looks like we have a lot to talk about."

Chase watched him go, and then teased her cell phone out of her pocket.

"You want something?"

"No, thanks, I'm fine," she replied as she stared at the screen. It wasn't a call that Chase had missed, but a message.

And it wasn't from Brad or Agent Stitts.

It was from Floyd of all people, and it was a single word: *ALONE*.

"What the hell?" she grumbled.

"What's that?" Martinez hollered from behind the wall.

"Nothing, just talking to myself."

Why did Floyd send me this? Is it—

Chase realized that while the message was just that single word—*ALONE*—there was a video attached to it. She raised her eyes and tilted her head to one side to determine if she could see Martinez from her vantage point.

She couldn't; he was out of sight.

"You sure you don't want anything? It'll help with the hangover. How about a Bloody Mary?"

"No, I'm fine, thanks," Chase repeated. She switched the volume off on her phone and then clicked the video.

It was grainy, but the time and date stamp in the bottom corner made it clear that it was security camera footage of some sort. Confused, Chase brought the screen closer to her face.

"I've seen pretty much everything, and I've had many partners over the years, some good, some bad, some pretty much terrible. I can tell you one thing, however: the only time I've really had a problem with a partner is when they weren't honest. Honesty and support, that's the key to a good, working relationship."

Chase listened to Martinez with half an ear as she watched the video progress.

It looked to have been taken from a bar of sorts, but the black-and-white footage gave no other hints as to where it was from.

Why did Floyd send me this?

Two women suddenly entered the scene, one dressed in a white jumper that came to well above her knee, the other a dark, low-cut blouse that matched her skin tone.

Chase inhaled sharply.

It was Yolanda Strand and Francine Butler, and they were laughing, arms locked, a drink in their free hand.

And they were *alive*.

It was security footage from inside The Barking Frog.

"What happened last night… that was a mistake, I know that, and I think you know that, too. But that's fine, we're both adults, we can get over it. That's not what concerns me."

Chase watched as a hooded figure approached the two girls. She could only see his back in the video, but she could tell by his posture that it was a man. He must have said something, because Yolanda unexpectedly threw her head back and laughed. But when the man held something out to them, something that looked like a small, black wallet, Yolanda grew serious again.

Chase watched as Francine started to frown, then she quickly set her drink on the bar. Yolanda did the same, and then the hooded figure left the shot, and the two girls followed.

Chase felt her heart skip a beat, knowing that these were the last images of the two girls taken while they were still alive.

The video stopped, and Chase immediately started it again from the beginning, watching more closely this time.

Who are you? she silently asked the hooded figure.

"What I'm really worried about is lack of honesty." Martinez said from behind the partition. "Have you been completely honest with me, Chase? I mean, from the beginning?"

"Y-yeah, of course. Honesty is very important," Chase replied absently, her attention still locked on the screen.

Yolanda was smiling, laughing, as was Francine. Until the man showed them something.

Chase paused the video. There was something here, something she wasn't seeing. It wasn't the thing the man was holding out to the girls, the video was far too small and grainy for her to make it out, but there was something…

"Hey, Martinez?" she asked in a soft voice.

"Yeah?"

"Did you ever hear back from Chief Downs about the video surveillance from The Barking Frog?"

There was a pause, which was broken by the sound of ice falling into a glass.

"It was deleted," Martinez informed her. "The bastard who owns the place, the fat one with the mustache and alopecia? He erased it before Downs could get a search warrant. Trying to protect Brent Pine, I guess."

Another pause.

"Why do you ask?"

Chase zoomed into the video still.

"No reason. Just wondering if there was any way that we can link the two crimes, is all."

The sigh from behind the wall was so loud it sounded almost pained.

"Let it go, Chase. Seriously. I was a rookie once, I know what it's like. You want to have a reason for everything, a motive. You think, or want, everything to be linked, to be connected. But you can't apply rational logic to wholly irrational acts made by unstable people. You know those magic squares? I used to love them as a kid… like a Sudoku starter kit, you know? Well, it's like trying to solve the squares using letters instead of numbers. It just doesn't work. Let it go."

Chase was barely listening now.

She blinked three times and brought the screen right up to her face.

The sleeves of the man's dark sweatshirt were rolled up, and there was something on one of his forearms, the one that held out the badge or wallet or whatever it was.

Chase shook her head, rubbed her eyes, and refocused her attention.

And then her blood ran cold.

The image was distorted at this magnification, but it was clear enough to make out an outline of a tattoo.

A tattoo that depicted a snake devouring an eyeball.

Chapter 39

ADRENALINE FLOODED CHASE'S SYSTEM. The first thing she did was check her holster, confirming that the gun that Martinez had given her was still there. The second thing she did was reply to Floyd's message, typing so quickly that she made several typos: *Floid, need FB Agent Jerey Stitts adres ASAPP.*

She cleared her throat, and when Chase spoke next, she called on all her poker skills, recalling every single time she had bluffed, every occasion that she had asked her opponent what cards he was holding in order to hear any change in the timber of his voice.

"You're probably right, Martinez, probably right. You know what?"

"What's that?"

"I think I might have that drink after all."

Martinez leaned out from behind the wall, a smirk on his face. Chase returned the expression.

"Seriously?"

"Sure, what the hell."

"What'll you have then?"

Chase thought about this for a moment. She needed something that would take some time to make, giving her just a little while longer to figure out what in the fuck it all meant.

Martinez was there? With the girls? On the night they were murdered?

"Well, you offered a Bloody Mary, so I guess I'll go with that. Extra spicy."

Martinez chuckled and moved back behind the wall.

"Sure thing."

Chase silently rose to her feet and scanned the room. She wasn't sure what she was looking for, but she knew that she would find something that would help her make sense of all this. Chase moved to Martinez's jacket, which hung on the back of his chair. She reached into the first pocket but found nothing. Then she checked the second. Inside, she found the evidence bag that Martinez had taken from Oren's restaurant.

Why does he have this? Why did he take it? Did he just forget to hand it back to Detective Jasper?

Chase tried not to crinkle the bag as she stared at the plastic inside. On it was a design of sorts made with a sharpie, but split down the middle as it was, there was no way to—

Chase folded the bag and the image suddenly made sense.

It was the same symbol, the same snake eating the eye on the forearm of the man in the video... on Martinez's forearm.

It can't be...

Heart racing, Chase slipped the evidence bag back into Martinez's jacket pocket, and then moved back to the bed. As she did, her eyes fell on the table by the corner of the room.

It was empty, but it hadn't always been that way.

Last night, there had been a plane ticket on it. A ticket and a receipt. Chase hadn't thought much about it at the time, but now...

The ticket had been for Martinez's flight out of Alaska to Logan International in Boston, but that in itself wasn't what finally sealed it for Chase.

It was the time.

Not of the flight, but on the receipt. Although Detective Jasper had pegged Oren and Julie's murders as taking place a day before they arrived, Chase hadn't been as certain. But without the hands, she hadn't been able to generate an accurate estimate.

But what she did know is that Agent Martinez had taken the call back in Anchorage around four in the afternoon. Only his receipt indicated that his ticket to Boston had been purchased at one, *before* the call came in.

Martinez had already been in Anchorage when Francine and Yolanda had been murdered, and now it appeared that he had, in the very least, planned to come to Boston before Oren and Julie were abducted.

These facts, along with the tattoo, were simply too big a coincidence for Chase to overlook.

Her mind suddenly flashed back to Anchorage when she had approached the white van that had housed Francine and Yolanda until their feet were chopped off.

Martinez had received a phone call just as they opened the van door. It had seemed off to her at the time, and the more she thought about it now, the more fake it seemed.

As if there was no one on the line.

And how quick he had been to accept that Brent the bartender had been their killer…

"Extra spicy, you said?" Martinez asked from behind the wall.

"Yeah," Chase replied softly.

Why? Why the fuck did he do this? Why did he kill those girls? Oren and Julie? Why would an FBI—

"Well, here it is," Martinez exclaimed, stepping out from around the corner.

Chase looked up at the man and instantly froze.

He was smirking and held an outstretched hand in her direction. Only it wasn't holding any drink.

Instead, Martinez was gripping the butt of a pistol.

Chase instinctively reached for the gun in her waistband, but Martinez's face went hard.

"Don't even think about it."

Chase swallowed and held her hands up.

"You know, Stitts said that you were good, but you… you're not *just* good," he looked skyward. "It would have taken Jeremy a month to figure it out, if at all, but not you. It took you… what? Two weeks? Less?"

Chase said nothing. She just stared, her mind working a mile a minute trying to figure out how she was going to get out of here alive.

How not to end up like Francine or Yolanda.

Or Oren or Julie.

"Calm down, Martinez, I—"

Martinez kept on talking as if she hadn't spoken.

"You almost got me, too. But you made a fatal error. Last night… you remember last night, right? Oh, I bet you do. Last night at the bar, you said that you're a beer girl, beer and maybe scotch. Not one for the mixed drinks, like Bloody Mary, and especially—"

The phone in Chase's pocket suddenly buzzed and Martinez's eyes dropped for a split second.

Chase bolted.

She sprinted for the door, yanking it wide. She moved quickly, but no one was fast enough to outrun a bullet.

Chase almost made it into the hallway before the first gunshot rang out.

She screamed as the bullet tore through the red parka and struck her just above the right hip.

Her legs threatened to buckle, but Chase knew that if she went down, she would never get back up again.

Gritting her teeth, Chase forced herself to stumble forward, to stay on her feet. And then, somehow, she managed to just keep on running as shots followed after her.

Chapter 40

WHEEZING, CHASE SLAMMED HER palms against the stairwell door. A siren sounded as it flung open, but she didn't know if it was a security alarm on the door or a fire alarm.

But Chase didn't rightly care.

Martinez was still after her, and he was going to kill her.

With one arm wrapped protectively around her stomach, her hand sticking to the down feathers that spilled from the hole in the jacket, she took the stairs two at a time, her heels barely touching one step before sliding onto the next.

She could hear muffled shouts from behind each of the doorways that she passed but continued without stopping. When she finally reached the bottom, Chase pulled her arm away from her stomach to slam both palms into the door marked EXIT.

All she got for her efforts was sore wrists.

"Shit!" she swore.

Footsteps echoed down from above.

"Chase! Get back here, Chase! Don't you want to know my motive? Huh? Don't you wanna know why?"

Chase's eyes darted around, and she saw a fire alarm beside the door. With blood-smeared fingers, she reached out and pulled it.

A bell rang, the sound so loud that it made her mind swim.

"*Chase! Chase!*"

Martinez's voice brought her back from the brink.

With both hands, she shoved the door again and, this time, it flung open. The cold air that blasted her in the face further shocked her into lucidity. It took Chase a split second to realize that she was in the back parking lot of the *W*, before she started to sprint across it, looking for something, anything that was familiar.

A police car, maybe, or a—

And then she saw it: a teal-colored sedan.

Paul sat inside, a cigarette dangling from his lips, his face buried in his phone.

He never even looked up as she approached.

With the hand not gripping her burning stomach, Chase reached behind her and pulled out her pistol.

"Get out!" she screamed. Paul's eyes snapped up, and the cigarette fell from his mouth. "Get out of the fucking car!"

But Paul didn't get out of the car; in fact, he didn't do anything at all, aside from shuttle his eyes from the pistol, to her face, to her torn parka. He yelped suddenly, and then swatted at the cigarette that burned his crotch.

Chase didn't hesitate; she grabbed the door handle and yanked it wide.

"Get out!"

Chase grabbed him by the collar as she shouted, and Paul, so confused and worried about the still-burning cigarette, did exactly as she asked.

Chase gave him a weak shove, then hopped into the car, slamming the door closed behind her.

She groaned when pain flared up her side but managed to slam the already running car into drive without wasting any more time.

Chase sped out of the parking lot without so much as a glance in the rearview mirror.

***

Chase pulled the phone from her pocket, intent on opening the message she had received in the hotel room, the one that had distracted Martinez enough for her to get away, but all she ended up doing was smear blood across the screen.

"C'mon!" she cried, wiping the phone on her jacket.

She managed to open it on a second try.

As expected, it was from Floyd, and as before, it was a simple message.

Not a single word this time, but an address.

Stitts's address.

Somehow, she managed to copy the address and drop it into the map program with one hand.

Then she dialed 9-1-1.

"9-1-1, what's your emergency?"

"Yes, it's FBI Special Agent Chase Adams, I need to speak to Detective Tim Jasper."

Chase took a hard left and then, for the first time since fleeing the parking lot, glanced up in the rearview. The map program instructed her to continue straight for seven miles, which wasn't ideal.

If Martinez was after her, and she expected that he was, then it would be easy to follow her.

"Agent Adams, what's your badge number?" the female 9-1-1 operator asked.

Chase scowled.

Badge number?

Her mind flashed to her badge that she had left in her hotel room before going to visit Martinez.

"I—I don't know," she said quickly. "Please, I need to speak to—"

"One moment please."

The phone clicked and for a second, Chase thought that the operator had hung up on her. A sudden, buckling pain gripped her entire right side and she cried out in agony.

Her body instinctively contracted in that direction, pulling the steering wheel to the left. The car veered into oncoming traffic, and someone blared their horn.

Chase righted the vehicle just as a male voice came through the telephone.

"Agent Adams?"

She recognized the voice immediately.

"Jasper! Jesus, you need to help me. Martinez… Martinez killed Oren and Julie and he killed those girls back in Alaska. He shot me, too… he fucking shot me—"

"Slow down, Chase."

"He shot me in the hotel room, I think the bullet went through, but—"

"Slow down."

"I think he's after me. Martinez is sick, demented—"

"*Slow down!*"

Chase finally took a deep breath.

"You've got to help me."

"I intend to—but you need to slow down. Where are you right now?"

Chase glanced outside at the bright sun, the cars passing by.

"I'm driving… I don't know exactly where, staying on 93. I'm heading toward—"

Chase hesitated.

"Yeah? Where're you going?"

Instead of answering right away, she chewed her bottom lip.

Again, Chase had the feeling that something just wasn't right.

In Alaska, Martinez was buddy-buddy with Chief Downs; knew him well. In Boston, he was pals with Jasper.

And Paul, the driver.

What had Martinez said back in the hotel room?

Something about rookie agents always needing a motive…

In this case, though, Chase was certain there *was* a motive, although she had no idea what the hell that was.

But why? Why is he doing this?

"Chase? You still there? Why don't you tell me where you're headed, and I'll pick you up. Better yet, come on in down to the station. It's not far. I can take you to the hospital, get the bullet wound in your stomach looked at."

"I'm going—"

Again, Chase paused.

…the bullet wound in your stomach…

She hadn't told Detective Jasper that the bullet had hit her stomach.

"Shit!" she swore.

Martinez had already gotten to the man already—he had his fingerprints on everything.

"Chase? Everything okay? Just tell me where you are—"

Chase glanced quickly at the cell phone and memorized the directions to Stitts's house. Then she rolled down the window and tossed her cell phone on the road.

They were going to trace it, probably already had.

Chase couldn't trust Jasper or his men.

She couldn't trust anyone but Stitts… but maybe this was just wishful thinking.

Please tell me that Martinez hasn't already gotten to Stitts, too.

Chapter 41

CHASE HAD NO IDEA how Martinez found her, but when she turned onto Arlington Road, she spotted a sleek, black car gaining on her.

His car.

The best course of action would have been to change her route, maybe even to head somewhere other than Stitts's house.

Only, she couldn't do that.

Chase had lost so much blood already that she was having a hard time even remembering the directions. Her entire shirt was soaked with the tacky substance, as was the inside of the red coat.

And to make things worse, she had started to feel dizzy over the past five minutes or so.

Just five more minutes, five more minutes and I'll be at Stitts's house, and he'll help me.

But both of those things were a lie, and deep down, she knew it.

Without her phone, she had no idea how much longer it was to Stitts's place, or even if she had remembered the directions correctly.

And when she got there? Who's to say that he would actually be home?

After all, she had tried to call him, what? A dozen times over the past few weeks? Two dozen?

And he had never answered. Not once. Hadn't returned her calls either.

There was also the distinct possibility that Martinez had already gotten to him, the way he had gotten to Downs and Jasper and...

Chase drifted into unconsciousness for less than a minute before her eyes snapped open again.

The tree was so close that she had no chance to avoid it. The only thing she could do was slam on the brakes, hoping that when she struck it, it wouldn't kill her on impact.

Her neck swung forward when the sedan smashed headlong into the tree. The airbag didn't discharge properly, probably owing to the age of the vehicle, and it only slowed her forehead before striking the steering wheel. Darkness threatened to overcome her again, but she fought it with all the might she had left.

Passing out again would mean certain death.

Martinez was after her and he would lop off... what? Her head? Her arms? Legs?

She refused to give him the satisfaction.

Chase unclicked her seatbelt, leaned over the passenger seat and tried to shove the door open.

It was jammed.

Wheezing, trying to ignore the pain in her side and now in her head, Chase somehow managed to turn herself around to drive both feet into it.

With a metallic groan, the door swung open just as two headlights filled the car.

Grunting loudly, fighting the spins and the pain that gripped her, Chase somehow managed to crawl across the seat.

And then she fell.

The tree that the car had struck lined an embankment, and when her body spilled from the vehicle, it immediately started to slide.

Chase tried her best not to scream, but she had already lost all control.

Part III - Trying to Shoot

PRESENT DAY

Chapter 42

"Oh, that's right. I know all about little Felix and Brad. You see, Chase, I've been at this a long time, and you don't stick around in this game by not knowing everything, all the facts... even about the victims."

Chase closed her eyes again, only this time it wasn't from the pain, but from the weight of Martinez's words. She ground her teeth so hard that a fine powder rained down on her tongue.

A game... that's all it is to him, a fucking game.

"Last chance, Chase. Come out now, hands up, or Felix and Brad die before you do. Last... chance..."

Chase grunted and shifted her weight to the side opposite the gunshot wound.

She closed her eyes, and images of Brad standing at the landing, his face half-covered in shaving cream flashed in her mind. And then she pictured Felix and the countless times she had arrived home from work and had slipped silently into his bedroom to kiss his blond head.

Tears slipped from her eyes.

Chase could hear Martinez somewhere on the road above and knew that he was about to make his way down to her. And then she would be put to a decision.

And if he didn't? Even if he stayed up there all night, she would have to do something soon; Chase didn't know how long she could go before the pain in her side, combined with the blood loss, would put her down for good.

"You know, Chase, I was just going to kill you the night you came into my room," Martinez continued. He let out a soft grunt, and she knew that he was starting toward her now. Chase flattened herself as much as possible beneath the culvert. "You woke up, remember? You turned to me. I don't know if you realized it, but I was cleaning my gun then, and I was going to kill you. Shit, if I'd known that you were going to put up such a fight... well, I would've just done it then."

The word *gun* resonated with Chase and she reached behind her.

It was still there.

She had no idea how it was possible, but the gun that Martinez had given her was still jammed in the holster. She was surprised that it hadn't fallen off during her sprint from the hotel, the altercation with Paul, and then the crash.

But it hadn't.

With a grunt of her own, she grabbed it and pulled it free.

Now we're even.

"To be honest, I'm not sure you're worth the trouble, Mrs. Adams. I mean, the other girls—those pieces of shit Yolanda and Francine, they begged and begged, but they didn't put up a fight. Oren, he was different. Heh, he tried to give up his girlfriend, Julie, tried to convince me to just take her. Real winner that guy. But you..."

Chase heard Martinez shuffle now, and her breathing quickened when he stopped just above her.

"You... meh, I guess it's fitting. Just you and my ex-partner Stitts to go. And then—"

Chase squeezed her eyes tight for a moment, and took a deep breath. Then, with one final groan, she pushed herself away from the side of the embankment, sliding out backward, gun raised in front of her.

Martinez's mouth turned into a wide O of surprise, and she realized that he wasn't just near the culvert but was actually standing *directly* on top of it.

This shocked her as well, but not nearly as much as it did Martinez.

Chase didn't hesitate.

She pulled the trigger three times, one after another.

She wasn't the best marksman, but she was good. Good enough to hit a man with all three bullets at this range.

But even though Martinez leaned backward, she never saw him recoil from impact.

There was something wrong.

The shots… they felt hollow. The gun wasn't that different from the one that she had trained on back in Seattle: a Glock 22. Granted, it had been a while since she had fired a gun, and yet this was… *different*.

She had no time to contemplate this further, however, because after the ringing faded from her ears, she heard something else.

Laughter.

Special Agent Martinez was laughing.

And he was still coming for her.

Chapter 43

CHASE RAN. SHE RAN through the woods and stomped through the snow, until her breath was coming in ragged gasps and her lungs were burning.

Although Martinez's motives were still a mystery, he was nothing if not determined. She knew that he wouldn't stop.

He wouldn't stop coming for her until one of them was dead. What had he said?

The rookie agent always wants a motive, a reason…

She didn't know if this had just been a strategy to throw her off, but it had been a lie. At least in his case.

There was a motive here… this had been meticulously planned. All of it, from Yolanda and Francine to Oren and Julie to… *her.*

Martinez had waited for his friends to be in power, in charge—first Downs then Jasper—so that he could move freely, so that he could make sure that it would end up looking like the bartender did it, like a junkie had gone mad and tossed the bodies into the river.

Out of breath, Chase put her hand on a large oak tree and moved around the other side. Then she lowered herself to the snowy ground.

Coming or not, Chase had to inspect her wound. She listened closely, and when she heard nothing other than the sound of croaking branches, she unzipped her jacket with a wince.

"Shit," she swore.

The right side of her blouse was dark with blood, and there was a half a dozen down feathers clinging to it.

She picked these away carefully, then inspected her wound through the thin streams of light that filtered through the trees. Chase had no idea what time it was, how much time had passed since she had left the hotel, but it appeared as if the sun was well into its daily voyage toward the horizon.

The good news was that the bullet appeared to have gone directly through her. The bad was that it was starting to smell, which meant that it had punctured her intestines. It could have been worse; had the bullet struck a lung, she likely wouldn't be walking now, let alone running through the woods.

Chase put her fingers next to the wound and pressed gently.

She grunted, and her abdominal muscles contracted. Fresh blood seeped from the bullet hole.

She needed to stop the bleeding.

Chase grabbed a fistful of snow and took another deep breath. She packed it tightly against the exit wound and then, before she lost her nerve, did the same with where the bullet had entered.

The sensation instantly sent an icy blast up and down her body, one that made her breath, which had since steadied, go ragged again.

She put her head back against the tree, and closed her eyes.

A moment before she passed out, something that Floyd had said to her what seemed like years ago came rushing back.

Martinez had a sister… but she died… was murdered.

And that, Chase knew, was the key.

The motive that she had been searching for all this time.

Chapter 44

"COME ON, DON'T BE shy. I just couldn't live with myself if you guys got heatstroke or something. So, get in. Like I said, I've got A/C in here."

Chase put her arms over her sister's shoulders and pulled her against her chest.

"Thank you, but we're fine just walking. I like the heat, anyway."

The man leaned further out the window and pulled the giant sunglasses down his nose.

Then he smiled, and for a moment, Chase considered getting into the van. She had heard about creepy men, stories her dad and her mom had told her, things that had been repeated at school, and how to avoid them. But this man… a man with a smile like that? With perfect teeth, and kind eyes? He even had the tiny creases in the corners like dad did. He couldn't be one of them, could he?

But then the man said something, something that made the tiny hairs on the back of Chase's neck stand on end.

"I'll take you right home, no stops. Promise."

Georgina pulled away from her. Not much, but just enough to cause Chase to tighten her grip on the girl's shoulders.

"Georgina," she whispered.

Chase wasn't sure if it was the heat getting to her, or if the act was inspired by her words, but her sister suddenly pulled away from her. The act took her by surprise and Georgina somehow managed to wriggle free of Chase's grasp.

"Georgina! No!" Chase cried.

In that moment, the van door opened, and the man stepped out. He was wearing a pair of blue overalls, Chase noted, and was much larger than she had first suspected.

In fact, he might have been the largest man she had ever seen, which is exactly what she would tell the police later.

"See? It's nice and cool in here," the man said, wrapping a meaty forearm over Georgina's shoulders.

The girl's eyes suddenly went wide.

"Chase? What—"

The man pulled a large knife from one of the many pockets in his overalls, and pressed the tip against Georgina's throat. The movement was so smooth, so fast, that it barely registered with Chase.

And all the while, the smile on his face never faded.

"Don't scream. Don't run and don't scream."

Georgina squirmed, but unlike Chase's, this man's grip was tight and strong.

Tears started to spill down her cheeks, turning her freckles into something that looked like mud streaks.

Chase felt her heart thud in her chest.

"Don't run. Don't scream," he warned again.

Chase wouldn't have known what to do if the man in the overalls hadn't told her. He wanted to be in control, and was letting her know exactly what he needed her to do in order to remain in power.

So Chase did the exact opposite.

She screamed as loud and as long as she had ever screamed before, even more than when her dad had broken the news that her dog Papi had been struck by a car and needed to be put down.

And Chase ran.

She ran as fast and as hard as her little legs could manage.

Chapter 45

CHASE AWOKE WITH A start. At first, she didn't know where she was, but when her breath exited her mouth in a frosty puff, everything came flooding back.

She glanced down at herself and realized that the snow that she had packed over the bullet hole had turned a pale shade of pink, but wasn't soaked red. The bleeding had slowed.

How long have I been out?

Having tossed her cell phone out the car window, she couldn't know precisely, but one thing was for certain: evening was upon them now.

A crunch of snow somewhere in the distance made her ears perk.

Fuck! He's still coming!

No matter what time it was, Martinez was still coming.

Chase held her breath and listened.

Nothing.

She was about to take another breath, maybe even sigh, when she heard the sound again.

It *could* be footsteps, but glancing around at the thin forest, it could also be a squirrel, a branch, or just the wind.

There was no way to tell.

Chase looked at the gun in her lap, and was about to open the chamber when she heard the sound for a third time.

She wasn't taking any chances. Stifling a groan, Chase pushed herself to her feet and started to run again.

Her first few steps were ungainly, her muscles stiff from the cold, her previous sprints down the embankment, and from sitting for as long as she had… however long that had been.

But she didn't look back.

Fueled by fear, she ran fast and hard, heading toward a dim yellow light tucked deep into the woods. It was too far and too dark to tell what the light was illuminating, but it *could* be a house.

It could be Stitts's house, for all she knew.

For all she hoped.

My ex-partner, Stitts, Martinez had said.

Chase couldn't believe it. No wonder he knew so much about her; Stitts must have told the man.

And yet, Stitts hadn't said a word about Martinez. When she had invited him to come and lend a hand in the Download Murder case, he had been flying solo.

She also remembered the way he questioned her, not in a condescending way, but gentle prodding, as if he was interviewing her not only to become an FBI Agent, but also to be his partner.

And yet for her first job, she had been paired up with the closet psychopath, Chris Martinez.

If the light was marking a house in the woods, and if by some stroke of sheer luck it was Stitts's place, then he might have known exactly where she was headed all along.

Chase could make out a faint outline of a log cabin beneath the light.

Martinez might know where she was headed now, but how could he have known where she would go immediately after leaving the hotel?

Unless…

Lost your luggage, did they? Happens. I've got an extra jacket you can use. A gun, too.

Chase swore under her breath, and she started to frantically pat her coat. The pockets were empty, as expected, but this didn't satisfy her. Still moving toward the log cabin, she felt around the seams, the zipper.

Her fingers pressed against something hard in the lining of the hood and she resisted the urge to curse out loud. Despite the cold, Chase peeled off the coat and tucked the pistol into the holster again.

Then she tore at the hood, peeling the red fabric apart at the seams. She yanked out a handful of down feathers and reached deep inside.

Her fingers found the hard object and she removed it.

It was a simple device, about the size of a half-dollar, with a small, jutting protrusion on one side.

Chase had seen similar electronics before. It was a tracking device, commonly used in computer bags and such. They usually worked on Bluetooth meshes, communicating with other objects that they passed in order to geolocate. In this case, though, Chase expected that this device was a little more sophisticated, probably working on a dedicated GPS link.

That fucking bastard…

Martinez had been tracking her ever since she got off the plane in Anchorage.

She thought back to when Floyd had driven her to the scene of Yolanda and Francine's murders.

Martinez had taken one look at her and hadn't hesitated: he had reached into his car and given her a jacket that he had at the ready.

Which meant that he must have known that Chase wouldn't have a coat.

Lost your luggage, did they?

"I bet he paid off the douchebag at the airport, too," Chase whispered.

Oh, Martinez had planned this alright.

Chase was about to throw the tracking device, but at the last moment thought better of it.

It might come in handy.

Besides, at this point, Martinez had to know that she was heading toward the house.

There was just nowhere else to go.

She just hoped that the man hadn't beaten her to it.

Chapter 46

CHASE PRESSED HER BACK against the wall beside the door, breathed deeply, and squeezed the gun in both hands.

The pain in her side had mostly subsided, but she knew that there would be more to come this day. With a deep breath, she reached over and tried the door.

It swung open without even needing to turn the handle.

Brow furrowed, Chase stepped inside, aiming the pistol first to her right, then to the left.

The interior of the cabin was much the way Chase expected based on the exterior: a plain, wooden rectangle. To her right was a modest kitchen, complete with an old-fashioned fridge and stove. To the left was a fireplace, the final remnants of logs reduced to embers. On the back wall was another door, leading to what she suspected was a rear porch.

Beyond the fireplace were two rooms, the doors of which were closed.

There was no sign of Martinez or any other occupants.

Chase, eyes still narrowed, slid deeper into the cabin, keeping the gun pointed out in front of her.

She moved quickly, noting a spot of blood on the floor near the fireplace. Instinctively scanning the fireplace tools, she noted that while the shovel was there, as was the broom, the slot she suspected that had once held the poker, was now empty.

Chase pressed up against the wall next to the first door. Then she reached over, turned the door handle, and threw it wide.

After waiting for a three count, she crouched low and spun in front of the opening.

It was a bathroom, and it was empty.

Chase turned to the other door next, and repeated the same process to clear this room.

Only this one took longer on account of it not being empty.

"Stitts!" Chase couldn't help but cry.

The man was sitting on the floor, his back pressed up against one of the large posts of a regal, and very much out of place, bed frame.

His head drooped low, a dirty rag wrapped around his mouth and head. His hair, usually perfectly cropped and styled, was damp and hung over his forehead in clumps.

He was shirtless, and his chest was marked with blood from numerous slashes.

Chase rushed to him, forgetting about Martinez altogether, and crouched on his level, fearing the worst. She set the pistol down, and then pulled the rag from Jeremy Stitts's mouth. He didn't gasp and sputter as she'd hoped.

"Stitts!" she repeated, pressing her fingers against the man's throat.

Relief washed over her; there was a pulse, but it was faint.

Only then did Chase realize that the man's arms were bound behind his back and around the wooden bedpost.

Working quickly, she tried to untie the ropes, but they were too complex too loosen by hand.

Especially given that she had no time.

Other than the wounds on his chest, which appeared at least on the surface to be superficial rather than intended to kill, there appeared to be nothing else wrong with him.

Chase rose to her feet. As she did, a chime—a miniature bell, maybe—sounded behind her, and she immediately bent back down and reached for the gun. With the familiar heft in her hand, she spun on her back while turning.

Pain engulfed her right hip, and she felt something deep inside the bullet hole, which had almost completely stopped bleeding, tear.

"No!" a voice cried, and Chase's finger relaxed on the trigger.

It was a dog, an aging Beagle that sauntered through the open door. It stopped, inspected her for a moment with rueful eyes, and then plunked itself down on the floor at Chase's side.

She took a deep breath, then turned to Stitts. He was awake now, his blue eyes, dull and bloodshot, boring into her.

"You're alive," she gasped.

Somehow, the man managed a grin.

"And you almost shot my dog," he said.

Chase sighed so completely that her entire body shuddered. For the past two weeks, she had had nobody she could speak to, nobody she could trust.

But now she had Stitts.

The tears came unexpectedly.

"Chase, you alright?" Stitts asked.

The question made Chase chuckle; despite everything that had happened, she actually chuckled.

Was she *alright, asks the shirtless, bleeding man bound to a post.*

Chase wiped her eyes and nose with the back of her hand.

No, I'm not alright, she wanted to say. Instead, she went with, "I'll live, but we need to get out of here. He's coming."

Stitts's eyes went wide.

"Martinez? He's here?"

Chase shook her head.

"No, not yet. But he's coming. Followed me through the woods."

Confusion washed over Stitts's face.

"He... what? He followed you? How did he—"

Chase straightened.

"He's my partner."

If Stitts had looked confused before, now his face collapsed into sheer wonderment.

"W—what? What the hell are you talking about?"

Chase, regaining her senses, started to look about the room for something to cut Stitts's bindings. There was no time to get into everything that had happened since Martinez's phone call, but Chase needed answers, too.

"Did he do this to you?" she asked.

"He came about a week ago, surprised me, tied me up. But... but how do you know him?"

Chase made her way slowly toward the bedroom door, her eyes on the kitchen.

"He's my partner," she repeated. The words sounded strange coming out of her, given everything that had happened. Eventually she spied a butcher block beside the stove. It was empty, but she made her way toward it anyway.

"But—but Chase, Martinez was booted from the Agency six months ago," Stitts's voice followed after her and Chase froze mid-step. "He failed his psych exam for the third time, and they had no choice but to put him on permanent leave."

Chapter 47

"*He what?*"

"He was let go, Chase. I have no idea how or why he came to you, or how he managed to—"

"He called me, told me that I was on a case, that I was to be his partner," Chase replied quietly. "Two girls murdered in Alaska."

"Alaska? Jesus, tell me... tell me, were the girls college aged?" Stitts asked desperately.

Chase nodded, still trying to wrap her head around the idea that Martinez was no longer with the FBI.

It would, in the very least, explain him not telling her about the higher ups or protocol. Martinez wanted to keep everything in house, with him, including working with Jasper and Downs—men that he knew well, men who wouldn't question his affiliation with the FBI as they had worked together previously.

Chase shook her head and closed her eyes.

"Chase? Were the girls—"

"Yes," she said softly. "They were in college."

Visions from Yolanda's perspective, of being in the van, of being terrified, flooded Chase's mind.

Terrified of Martinez—Francine and Yolanda had been terrified of *him*.

He sawed off their goddamn feet and then kept them alive so that they would freeze to death.

"His sister's friends," Stitts whispered.

Chase, still frozen partway to the kitchen, turned and looked at him. His face had regained some color, but it was clear that he hadn't eaten or had anything to drink for some time, which explained his weak pulse.

"What do you mean?" she demanded. "His sister—"

The beagle, who up until this point had been lying on its haunches, its dopey eyes staring up at Chase, suddenly raised its head. Chase stopped speaking and listened. Stitts did the same.

Although she heard nothing, something had piqued the dog's interest.

Martinez was close.

Chase hurried to the kitchen and threw the drawers open. Inside the first one, she found forks and spoons as well as several steak knives.

She grabbed one of the knives and hurried back to Stitts. Without saying a word, she bent and started to saw at the ropes. It took several tries, but eventually she managed to cut through.

Stitts groaned as he brought his arms in front of him and started to rub his wrists.

Chase had been leaning over the man as she sawed at the rope, and when she pulled away, she realized that Stitts's left shoulder was covered in blood.

Stitts must have noticed, too, as before he stood, he looked her over.

"Jesus Christ, you've been shot," he gasped.

Chase looked down at herself as if this was some sort of new revelation.

Her entire side was wet with fresh blood. Whether her reaction was psychosomatic or real, it was one thing: visceral.

Chase swooned and fell to one knee. At the same time, Stitts rose on wobbly legs and helped her back to her feet. They braced each other.

The beagle also rose to its feet, but Chase couldn't tell if it was because it had heard something or was only responding to them.

"We have to get you to a hospital," Stitts said.

Chase shook her head.

"Martinez is coming."

"Which means we have to hurry," Stitts barked as he tried to guide her toward the door.

Chase took a deep breath and grounded herself. Then she leveled her eyes at Stitts.

Yolanda Strand and Francine Butler didn't get a chance to go to the hospital. They had had their feet lopped off and then were stripped naked and left to freeze to death. Oren and Julie had their hands removed before being thrown into the water.

They didn't get a chance to go to the hospital.

"No," Chase said. "This ends here."

Chapter 48

"**I've got five rounds** left," Chase told Stitts.

Stitts looked at the gun in her hand.

"That your pistol?"

Chase shook her head.

"No, mine was lost at the airport."

Even as the words left her mouth, she knew what was coming next.

"Where'd you get this one from?"

"Martinez gave it to me," Chase replied hesitantly.

Stitts swore and reached for it. Chase handed it over and he immediately popped the round from the chamber.

Stitts held it in his palm for a moment before showing it to Chase.

"No, you don't have five rounds left," he said.

Chase scrunched her brow, trying to understand what he was telling her. Then she noticed the crimped bullet top.

"Fucking blanks," she spat.

And that's why I missed Martinez when I fired three shots center mass.

"Shit."

Stitts closed his palm around the shell and chewed his lower lip.

"It'll still make a bang, though," he said, apparently to himself. He ejected the magazine, removed three of the four other blanks and walked over to the microwave. He put them on the tray, then set the dial on high for five minutes.

Chase simply stared.

The beagle sauntered over to her and rubbed up against her leg. Chase pulled away with a gasp, which caused fresh pain to shoot up her side.

First the jacket, now the gun. First the—

An idea suddenly came to her. She started to take her jacket off, but when it came to her right side, she was unable to shake it free.

Stitts lent her a hand.

"What's going on?"

"Put it on," Chase instructed.

Stitts looked at her, but didn't resist; he was, after all, shirtless and the fire in the hearth was nearly out.

"What are you thinking?"

Now it was Chase's turn to pause.

"You and I know that the gun is filled with blanks, but Martinez doesn't know that we know."

Stitts stared at her. And then he grinned again.

"Let's get this bastard."

***

Alone in the dark, Chase was drawn back to a different time.

She was undercover as a narcotics officer, attempting to infiltrate a dingy crack house that also whored out underage girls.

Only it was Chase who was infiltrated. Memories of her sister kept haunting her, images of that fateful day when Georgina was taken, and when it came time to 'pretend' to take her first hit, Chase just couldn't resist.

"You see?" Tyler said, *"It doesn't matter what your problems are, a little brown sugar always makes things right."*

An incredible warmth washed over her then, not hot and uncomfortable, just perfect *warmth*. Once, Chase had spent a half hour in a flotation tank, in which the water and the air were the exact same temperature as her skin. It felt like that, except she didn't have any of the anxiety associated with being trapped in a bubble. And then there were the fingers… it felt as if every inch of her body was being massaged by millions of tiny fingers.

Tyler was right.

As much as Chase hated to admit it, for the first time in nearly three decades, she didn't think about her sister, about the way the tears spilled from her eyes as the man in the van wrapped his heavy forearm over her chest and shoulders.

And it was this feeling, or lack thereof, that kept her coming back for more.

Part of her, a dark part that Chase had buried long ago, wanted some *brown sugar* now. Part of her, she knew, would *always* want some.

The sound of a door opening drew her back to the present.

"Chase! *Chaaaaaa-aaase!* Come out, come out, wherever you are."

Chapter 49

CHASE'S BREATH WAS COMING in shallow bursts as the footsteps approached.

She heard Martinez try the light switch, but the cabin remained dark. Chase had unscrewed the bulbs in the main room, leaving the only illumination the nearly burned out fire.

"Clever girl," Martinez said under his breath. The footsteps were lighter now, less pronounced, "Why don't you just come out and we can talk this through?"

Chase remained seated, arms behind her back, head low.

"I never expected for things to make it back here, to Jeremy's of all places, but it's only fitting, given that you two started all this."

Started this? We *started this?*

"I mean, you guys were both there with her, both had a chance to stop it. But you didn't, did you?"

She heard the bathroom door being thrown wide.

"Or maybe you're not even here anymore, Mrs. Adams. Maybe it's just you, Jeremy. But that's okay. I've waited a long time to avenge her death, and I can wait a little while longer to finish this. But mark my words, I will finish it."

Chase tried not to think too much about Martinez's words, and instead tried to prepare herself for the plan that she and Stitts had constructed.

The door to the bedroom was closed, and what little light eked in from beneath it darkened completely as Martinez stopped in front of it.

Chase held her breath as Martinez's knuckles brushed against the wood and it slowly started to open.

"Knock, knock, who's there."

Chapter 50

The light flicked on and Chase raised her eyes to stare at Martinez. The man was holding a pistol in one hand, a cell phone in the other, and his blue snow jacket hung open.

His hair was slick with sweat or snow and his eyes were squinted.

Chase had hoped to surprise the man by taking Stitts's place, but the only thing she saw on his handsome face was a combination of deep-seated anger and satisfaction.

Martinez opened his mouth to say something, but before he could speak, Chase leveled her own pistol at the man and started to shriek.

"Stitts! Now! He's here! *Come now!*"

Martinez tensed, but only for a second before his eyes darted to his cell phone.

He laughed.

"Ah, Chase Adams… Chaaaaaaaase Adams, you gave Stitts your coat, didn't you?"

Chase said nothing; she only scowled.

"Yeah, yeah you did. But here's the thing—" he turned the cell phone to her and she saw what looked like a map, "—I put a tracking device in the red jacket I gave you… and it looks like your man Stitts is long gone by now. Long, *long* gone."

Chase felt her jaw go slack. Between breaks in Martinez's words, she thought she had heard the electric thrum of the microwave start up.

"Why are you doing this?" she demanded, trying to keep Martinez talking so that he didn't pick up on the sound himself.

Martinez scowled.

"You still don't get it, do you? It took me years to set this up, to plan everything out perfectly. To avenge *her* death," he glanced at the cell phone. "It hasn't run as smoothly as I'd hoped, but it's almost over. If Stitts thinks he can make it to his four-by-four and then head into the city for help, he's sorely mistaken. I emptied the gas tank. It's going to get cold out there tonight, and jacket or not, he's going to have no choice but to come back here. And when he does, I'll be waiting. Waiting with you, Chase."

Another sharp intake of breath.

"You forgot one thing, Martinez," Chase said softly.

"Yeah, and what's that?"

"I've got a loaded gun aimed at your head, and I'm not afraid to pull the trigger."

Martinez laughed again.

"Stitts said that you were smart, but… but I'm beginning to think that maybe he overestimated you. Sure, you figured out that I was the one responsible for the murders, but maybe that was just a fluke."

"I don't know what you're rambling about, but you have three seconds to drop your gun before I start shooting."

"Oh, Chase, you think you can hit me? You already missed three times by the road. What makes you think you can hit me now?"

"It was cold outside, and I was bleeding. But I won't miss again. Not in here."

Martinez shook his head.

"You don't get it, do you? The gun is filled with—" *blanks*, she knew he was going to say, but he was interrupted by the sound of gunfire coming from the kitchen.

Chapter 51

MARTINEZ WHIPPED HIS HEAD around toward the sound of the shots, a curse on his lips. He led with the gun, and crouched as he spun.

Chase tried to stand, but the pain that gripped her side kept her seated. She could feel her blouse clinging to her cold flesh, and the waistband of her jeans was soaked through.

"Stitts! Did you—" Martinez shouted, but the gun powder in the final shell in the microwave went off, and this time, he ducked.

As he did, Agent Jeremy Stitts stepped from the shadows. He grunted as he swung the fireplace shovel in a wide arc, and it twisted in the air.

If it hadn't been for the last blank, the shovel would have surely struck Martinez directly in the face, knocking him out cold. But Martinez had ducked, and instead of smashing his nose and mouth, the corner struck him in the center of the forehead. It made a thick groove in his flesh, and dragged all the way to his eye, tearing his lower eyelid down.

Martinez shrieked, but while he staggered from the impact, he didn't go down.

"Stitts! Get him! Get him!" Chase yelled from her spot on the floor. Again, she tried to rise, but only raised a few inches before slumping back against the bed. The gun was heavy in her hand, and even though she knew there was only one round—a blank—in the chamber, she pulled the trigger anyway.

It clicked, but the round didn't go off.

"Stitts!" she screamed.

Stitts, sporting the red parka that was two sizes too small, lunged at Martinez, trying to take advantage of the other man's stunned state.

But Stitts had been strapped to the bed frame for god only knows how long; he was tired, beaten, and dehydrated.

Even if they had both been fully rested, Chase doubted that Stitts would have had much of a chance.

She knew that Martinez was heavily muscled, had seen his bare chest flexing as he thrust into her. And even though blood poured from his forehead and leaked into his deformed eye, Martinez managed to swat the second blow aside with his forearm. Stitts had put so much into this swing, that his body followed the trajectory and he stumbled.

And Martinez was on him.

"No!" Chase screamed. But screaming was all she could muster even as Martinez started to rain down punches on Agent Stitts.

"You let her *die!*" Martinez screamed as his fists collided with Stitts's face. "*You let her die! I told you she was out there, but you didn't believe me!*"

Blood was streaming from the cut on his forehead and sprayed from his lips.

Chase closed her eyes, trying to block out the sickening sound of first flesh on flesh, then bone on bone.

After several more dull thuds, the beating stopped, and Chase had no choice but to look again.

She watched as Martinez stood, his back heaving with deep breaths. He reached over and grabbed the shovel from Stitts's lifeless hand.

Chase felt tears spill down her cheeks, and she knew that this was the end.

Martinez walked toward her, his massive chest still heaving, his hands twitching slightly.

With blood covering half of his face, he looked like an animal who had just devoured his kill.

"It could have been easy, Chase," he said as he closed the distance between them. "It could have been so easy."

Without waiting for a response, he swung the shovel with one hand.

Chase heard a final thud, and this was the last thing she heard for a long time.

Chapter 52

"*I CAN MAKE YOU forget. I can make you forget everything, Chase. Just one hit... that's all you need to forget all about your sister, about what happened that day.*"

Chase felt herself nodding, and then she closed her eyes as the needle broke the soft skin on the inside of her elbow.

"*Brown sugar will make everything go away. Everything.*"

Chapter 53

CHASE'S EYELIDS FLUTTERED, AND she felt her arms being twisted behind her.

Her right side erupted in agony, which intensified when she was hauled to her feet.

"Stand up, Chase. This isn't over yet. But it will be… it'll all be over soon."

This time when Chase's eyelids fluttered, they didn't open.

Chapter 54

CHASE GASPED AS COLD water splashed her face.

She sputtered and shook her head. Instantly, her vision began to swim, and she felt an odd thickness to the right side of her cheek, as if someone had injected plasticine beneath her skin.

"Wakey, wakey," a male voice said. Shadows clouded her vision, and everything seen by her right eye had a pinkish tinge to it. But as she blinked, Chase finally began to make out a familiar shape.

Martinez's shape.

His forehead was still bleeding, and his right eye appeared to slump in the socket. She could see more of the white globe than she would have ever wanted.

Panic coursed through her, and she tried to shift her head and look around, to find Stitts's body, but her movements were restricted.

Martinez had bound her hands behind her and around the bedpost. He had also looped a rope around her neck.

As for Stitts, she could only see his legs, which remained motionless on the floor.

"You wanna know why?" Martinez asked suddenly, his tone changing to something softer.

Chase swallowed hard but offered no response. It was clear, however, that Martinez didn't require any encouragement.

"Anna Martinez… she was only twenty years old at the time, Chase. My beautiful sister was just *twenty*," his voice hitched, and he had to take several deep breaths before continuing. "And they gave up on her… the NYPD, Seattle PD, and the FBI. Shit, *the* FBI, the Agency I worked for, they gave up on her. Told me I couldn't get involved, conflict of interest and all that shit—that I was to stay out of it. Then they had the *fucking* nerve to tell me that she—that beautiful Anna—had traveled to New York, that she had become one of the Skeleton King's victims. What a fucking joke! My sister, dead at the hands of a serial killer... because why? They found a strand of her hair at the scene? Really? A single strand of hair?"

There were tears streaming down his cheeks, which mixed with the blood to give his face a pink sheen. Martinez brought his gun into full view and caressed her swollen jaw with the barrel.

Chase's mind was racing, trying to piece together the ramblings, to figure out what it all meant, and most importantly, how *she* fit into this picture.

"She was only twenty years old... just *twenty*. And they gave up on her. But I didn't, Chase. I didn't give up. I went looking, I did everything I could to find her, and you know what?"

He twisted his head to one side, showing her his gleaming eyeball.

"I found her. I fucking found her. I found what was left of my sister."

Martinez was so close that she could smell his sour breath, the reek of his blood.

Of *their* blood.

"Please, Chris, let me—"

Martinez silenced her by applying pressure to her jaw with the gun.

"That bastard, Tyler Tisdale got her addicted to heroin and whored her out until there was nothing left of her. I had no choice but to put her out of her misery." When he spoke next, his voice was but a whisper. "Imagine what that does to a man."

Chase's heart skipped a beat.

Tyler? Tyler Tisdale?

***

"Chase… just one hit. Trust me, if you like that other stuff, this is going to blow your mind."

Chase stared at the small baggie of the yellowish powder. Tyler was smiling, but not in a creepy way. He was smiling in a knowing way; a look that told her he knew she would try it.

Chase lowered her gaze.

"I know you want to forget, Chase, forget all about your sister," Tyler whispered.

Chase shut her eyes, trying to keep her tears at bay. But she couldn't. It might have been the lack of sleep or the exhaustion that finally broke her down, or maybe it was just the damn job. For a full month, she had been around the drugs, the girls with their eyes rolled back in their heads as a sweaty fat man lay on top of them, grunting and thrusting, and the whole time Chase could do nothing.

Spend enough time in this world, and you become part of it. A little bit of yourself is lost, a bit that can never be recovered.

Like that day, the day when the man in the van had taken Georgina. The day when Chase had turned her back and ran.

Without opening her eyes, Chase raised her arm and pulled back her sleeve.

"Help me," she whispered, tears still streaming down her cheeks. "Help me forget."

Chapter 55

"I TOLD YOU," AGENT Martinez hissed. "I told you that I did my research. I know all about you. I know that you were there."

Chase's entire body racked with sobs.

"I brought him in," she gasped. "I brought that bastard Tyler in."

He tried to do the same to me! I was a victim!

Martinez pulled away from her.

"Yeah, I'll give you that. You did. You brought him in, and he's rotting in prison because of you. I should be thanking you for that. But you were too late. Did you see her? Did you see my sister there? Whoring herself?"

Chase shut her eyes, but this didn't stop the images from flashing in her mind.

Images of the girls, some young, some old, eyes rolled back to the whites…

"I tried," she whispered.

Martinez laughed.

"Tried? *You tried?* Anna tried. She tried to get away. Just like Yolanda and Francine. They tried to get away, too. Don't you see? I researched all of you."

Chase finally opened her eyes.

"Yolanda? Francine?"

"They were her friends, or at least they claimed to be. They were the ones that told Anna to take her first hit, to get high at that fucking shitty Barking Frog. *Just one fucking hit*, they said. But it wasn't one hit for Anna, it never was. Never could be — Addictive personality, moderation didn't exist in her vocabulary. She did the exact same thing that they did, but they could stop. Anna couldn't. And do you know what they did when she got addicted?"

Chase tried to shake her head, but the binding around her throat was too tight to move. Martinez stormed back toward her, and Chase prepared herself for another blow that never came.

"They fucking abandoned her!" he shouted in her face. Blood and spit speckled her already damp cheeks. "They gave up on her, just like Jeremy Stitts did. He was my fucking partner for Christ's sake! And he bought it... bought the party line that she was a victim of a serial killer."

Martinez brought the gun up and tapped his chest.

"But I knew... I knew she was still out there. And she was *dying*. She was being killed, slowly, each and every day with a needle, with a fucking prick. And Stitts refused to listen, denied."

And there it was, the final piece to the puzzle.

Chase felt her chest tighten, and at first thought it was the wound again, but then realized it was something else.

Agent Stitts hadn't helped Martinez, and Yolanda and Francine had been there the first time Anna had taken a hit. Oren Vishniov and his partner Julie Cooper had sold them the drugs. Martinez hadn't said as much, but Chase could read between the lines.

And Chase... Chase had been there when Anna had been.

With Tyler.

Undercover.

But also addicted.

Emotion suddenly overwhelmed her.

"I'm sorry," she sobbed. "I'm—"

A flicked of movement from behind Martinez drew her eyes.

Stitts's legs were no longer visible.

Chase wanted to say more, to keep him talking, but Martinez brought something up in front of his face, something that took her breath away.

A saw.

The blade was speckled with dark brown stains, but Chase knew that this wasn't rust.

It was blood.

Francine's blood. Yolanda's blood.

Oren's.

Julie's.

And soon it would be hers.

Martinez brought the saw out in front of him now, the cold steel reflecting a shaft of wayward moonlight that had burrowed its way into the cabin.

"You're sorry? *You're sorry?* Well that makes it right then, doesn't it?"

Chase shook her head, no longer caring about the way the rope burned the smooth skin of her throat.

"No," she croaked. "It doesn't."

Martinez ignored her.

"I guess I'm sorry too, then," he said softly as he raised the saw to her neck.

Chase's eyes went wide.

"I'm really, really sorry. But, you see, I'm also sorry that when Anna cried out, there was no one there to listen. So, when *you* shout, no one will help you either. Yolanda and Francine? Anna tried to walk away. She couldn't. And so did those girls. Anna reached for help, just like Oren and Julie. But there was no one there to hold her hand, to get her. And you—you were there, undercover. And I bet she cried to you, cried every night as she was being raped by another nameless man just so that she could score another hit. And I bet—"

Agent Stitts suddenly appeared behind Martinez, his face a swollen, bruised mess.

He held her pistol in his hand, and slowly raised it.

The saw was cold against Chase's throat—impossibly cold. Her entire body felt frozen, spreading from the hole that the bullet had made when it had passed through her side to where the tine of the saw bit into her flesh.

"I'm sorry," Martinez said as he started to move the saw, and this time, he actually sounded remorseful.

Chase spotted Agent Stitts stumble toward them, saw him raise the gun, and she closed her eyes.

I'm sorry, too. I'm sorry that I let him take you, Georgie. I'm sorry that I ran and that you stayed.

She waited for the saw to slice through the soft skin under her chin, but when it didn't happen, Chase opened her eyes.

Martinez's face had gone slack.

"Put the—" Agent Stitts growled, but he never completed the sentence. Martinez started to turn, and as he did, Stitts squeezed the trigger.

The round might have been a blank, but that didn't matter. It was pressed up against the back of Martinez's skull, and when Stitts fired the gun, the room exploded.

As did the back of Martinez's head.

Warm blood sprayed Chase's face and she screamed.

She screamed even as Stitts tore her bindings away. She screamed as she fell to the ground.

She screamed when Stitts collapsed beside her.

Chase screamed until her entire world went black.

Chapter 56

CHASE AWOKE TO THE sound of a bell.

The bells at heaven's gate, she thought incoherently.

Something wet touched her face, and she grunted. Her entire body was sore, and she felt unable to move.

The wetness persisted, and Chase finally managed to open her eyes.

Stitts's beagle had returned and its rough tongue was lapping the side of her cheek.

She groaned and blinked, trying to clear her vision. Her movements caused the dog to pull away from her, and she heard the bell again, which drew her gaze.

A small smile crossed her lips when she saw the tracking device attached to the dog's collar.

Then reality struck, and the expression slid off her face.

Chase was lying on her side in a pool of blood, only about half of which appeared to be hers.

The rest was from the mess that was now the back of Martinez's head.

"Stitts!"

He was lying on his back, only three feet from her. His face was a swollen mess, and Chase had to stare hard to see his chest rise and fall.

But breathe he did; Stitts was alive, but for how long, she couldn't be certain.

Chase forced the pain from her mind and looked around.

There, not ten paces from where the three of them lay was Martinez's cell phone. It was still open to whatever map program he was using, and the tracker glowed red directly in the center of the screen.

Chase closed her eyes and breathed deeply.

Then she started to crawl.

The beagle was by her side the entire time, silently urging her onward with encouraging licks.

When Chase finally opened her eyes, she realized that she had crawled past the cell phone.

It was beside her shoulder and she reached out and grabbed it.

With one final, deep breath, Chase dialed 9-1-1 and brought it to her ear.

Epilogue

SIX MONTHS LATER

A KNOCK AT THE door drew Chase's eyes from the file. She lifted her head and waited. When the knock came a second time, she shut the file and then with a wince, rose from the kitchen table.

As she made her way to the front door, her gait became more fluid and the pain in her side started to fade.

Chase looked through the peephole, then pressed her back against the door and shut her eyes.

"I see your shadow, Chase," the man on the other side of the door told her. "I know you're in there. Open up, I've got someone here who wants to speak to you."

A smile touched Chase's lips and she opened her eyes. Then she turned, unlocked the door and pulled it wide.

Jeremy Stitts stared back at her. His face was mostly healed, and aside from a dimple, more of a dent, really, beneath his right eye, there was no other evidence that he had been beaten nearly to death.

He surprised Chase by leaning in and giving her a hug.

Chase embraced Stitts, relishing the first human contact she'd had from a person not in a white lab coat. And then a dog barked, and she pulled away.

With a grunt, she squatted on her haunches and scratched the beagle behind his ears.

"Good boy," she said. "Good boy."

Jeremy helped her to her feet.

"You never even told me the dog's name," Chase said as she led Jeremy toward the kitchen. "Damn mutt saved our lives, and I don't even know his name."

Jeremy snickered.

"First of all, it's a *she*, and *she* isn't a mutt."

Chase shook her head.

"Figures; if it had been a male dog, it probably would've messed up the plan."

Stitts faced her.

"Her name is Mia," Stitts said, suddenly growing serious.

Chase nodded and ran her fingers along the dog's back.

"Well, thank you, Mia. Thank you for saving our lives."

Before emotions overwhelmed her, Chase turned away and moved toward the counter.

"You want a coffee?"

"Sure."

Chase poured two cups, and then took a seat at the table across from Stitts.

Mia curled up at her feet.

Jeremy's gaze was on the plain manila folder, but he stopped staring when Chase caught his eye.

"How you holding up?" he asked.

Chase shrugged.

"Getting better. The wounds are mostly healed. The docs say it'll take a few more months for the muscles to be right again, but I should make a full recovery. And you?"

Chase stared at Jeremy Stitts's face as she spoke. The man was handsome, and he offered her a perfect smile as a response. He looked exactly as Chase remembered him from the first time they had met over a year ago in New York City.

Aside from the new dimple, of course.

"I'll be fine," he said. "But you... I don't only mean your physical wounds, Chase."

Chase couldn't hold his stare any longer.

"I'll be fine—been through worse."

"Yeah, that's what I'm worried about."

Silence fell over the three of them then, and Chase just let it play out as she sipped her coffee. She was aware that Jeremy was inspecting her the entire time but didn't take offense.

That was just how he was.

And if Chase was good at anything, it was keeping a poker face.

She finished her coffee and then said, "Are you done deposing me, Agent Stitts? Because, you know, I'm reeeeaaaaaaaally busy here."

Stitts finished his own cup and stood.

"You ready to get back to work, Chase? I mean, for real this time?"

Chase nodded.

"I'm ready."

"Give me a month, and then we'll get you down to Quantico for some orientation."

Chase made a mock salute.

"Aye, aye, Captain. But I have one condition."

Stitts grew serious again.

"Sure, what is it?"

"No psycho partners this time around, okay?"

Jeremy chuckled.

"Sorry, you're stuck with me. I'll see myself out." He clapped his hands and Mia jumped to her feet. "Come on, girl, Chase needs her rest."

He was nearly at the door when something that Martinez said occurred to her.

"Hey Stitts?"

He stopped and turned.

"Yeah?"

"Did you really say that I was naive, that I try to see the good in everyone?"

Stitts hesitated before answering.

"I'm not sure… do you?"

He didn't wait for a response.

Chase watched the two of them go, a smile on her face. When Stitts closed the door behind them, however, the smile vanished.

She reached into the pocket of her sweatshirt and pulled out an orange medicine container. Inside, she found one, solitary pill. Chase swallowed it dry, and then turned her attention back to the folder she had been reading before Stitts had interrupted her.

Ernest & Ernest Law Offices, the header read.

Her scowl deepened as she read the first few lines of text over and over again.

Brad was filing for divorce, and he was seeking full custody of Felix.

He had visited her in the hospital during her recovery, of course, and Felix had come along. And not once had he mentioned this. Now, when she was almost fully recovered, a bombshell was delivered by a court-appointed sleaze ball.

Chase threw the empty medicine container across the room, and then immediately cried out and clutched her right side protectively.

"Fuck!"

She collapsed on the ground and held her face in her hands as the tears started to flow.

Images flashed through her mind in rapid succession, first the man in the van with the aviator sunglasses, then Georgina's tearing eyes, then her first hit, Stitts, and finally

Martinez's face just as the blank exploded against the back of his skull.

And, behind all of this, there was a voice.

Chase managed to stand, and staggered down the hallway toward her bedroom. She threw the door open so hard that it dented the drywall.

With determined steps, fighting the pain from the sudden act of throwing the medicine bottle, Chase strode to her nightside table. She pulled the drawer out hard, yanking it entirely free and tossing it on the floor behind her. Then she snaked her hand in and ran it along the underside of the wooden top.

For a moment, panic set in when her searching fingers failed to find it.

"Where the—"

But her index finger brushed against something hard, and she carefully peeled the tape away.

Two items fell into her palm and she squeezed them tightly as she withdrew her hand.

For nearly a full minute, she just stared at her knuckles, which had begun to turn white.

With a deep breath, Chase unfurled her fingers, revealing a syringe with an orange cap and a small bag of off-white powder emblazoned with an icon of a snake devouring an eyeball.

Her brow furrowed for a moment and she tilted her head, examining the eye first, then the snake, then the image as a whole.

What did it mean? she wondered, but then the voice returned.

Tyler Tisdale's voice.

I can make you forget, Chase. I can make you forget everything.

END

Author's Note

Although I wrote FROZEN STIFF to be enjoyed as a standalone novel, if you want to learn more about Chase Adams and her past before getting that fateful telephone call, check out the Damien Drake series. If you just want more Agent Adams (how dare you play favorites with my children), the second book in this series—SHADOW SUSPECT—is now available. I also wanted to take a moment to offer an apology to everyone who pre-ordered this book: the original release date got pushed back by about a month. I try my best to honor the pre-order dates that I set, and when I put my books up for pre-order, I do so with the intention of getting them out on time. Sometimes, though… sometimes things just pop up. And what are these *things* you ask? Some are under my control—mainly, writing the book—while others—cover design, editing, proof reading, publishing—are not. Thank you, guys for sticking around.

2018 is going to be a great year, full of many books, including several more Chase Adams FBI Thrillers, the continuation of Damien Drake's saga, as well as the introduction to Dr. Becket Campbell's medical thriller series. I'm also toying with the idea of one more series set in this universe, but I'm not ready to reveal the star just yet…

And now we've arrived at the inevitable call-to-action: if you enjoyed this Chase Adams thriller, then please leave a review for FROZEN STIFF wherever you bought it from. Not only do reviews help other readers find books that they might like, but it also helps me decide what books to write next. So, please, log on to your favorite retailer, type a quick review, and get back to what you like doing best: reading, rearranging your sock drawer, or whatever else tickles your… umm, ear.

As always, if you have any comments, suggestions, or if a dastardly typo somehow managed to slip through the cracks, or if you just want to say hi, stop on by my Facebook page @authorpatricklogan or drop me an email at patrick@ptlbooks.com.

As always, you keep reading, and I'll keep writing.

Best,
Patrick
Montreal, 2017